MISTLETOE MYSTERY

Philly Sanderson is struggling to keep Bedlington Hall afloat. Even the murder weekends she runs with her best friends, Puck and Meg, are a failure. Then two things happen. She finds a painting in the attic, and she meets the drop-dead gorgeous Matt Cassell. Things seem to be looking up, but Philly soon realises that there are secrets at Bedlington Hall, and Matt is involved. Can she survive a Christmas of murder, mystery and mayhem with her heart intact?

SALLY QUILFORD

---◆---

MISTLETOE MYSTERY

Complete and Unabridged

LINFORD
Leicester

First published in Great Britain in 2011

First Linford Edition
published 2012

British Library CIP Data

Quilford, Sally.
  Mistletoe mystery. - -
  (Linford romance library)
  1. Love stories.
  2. Large type books.
  I. Title II. Series
  823.9′2–dc23

  ISBN 978–1–4448–1362–3

1

Supermodel Lucy Crystal smiled benignly as she chatted to the dinner guests, telling them her life story. Philly Sanderson could not help noticing that Lucy embellished a little. In a few minutes, Lucy would drink her coffee and then choke to death on the arsenic.

The sound of thunder and lightning filled the dimly-lit room, whilst a warm fire crackled in the hearth. The atmosphere at Bedlington Hall was just right for a murder.

Philly smiled with satisfaction and glanced at the other diners, who were busy looking at each other with deep interest, whilst finishing off their drinks. Things were going well so far. No one had guessed, which was good at this stage of the plot. The first time some know-it-all had turned up and ruined everything by guessing immediately what was going to happen. Luckily, Philly had talked her way out of it and changed the plans at the last minute, but it had taken a lot of doing in the time she had available to her.

Lucy's husband, a young vicar called Reg, sat opposite her. He was rather portly, with a red face. It had been an unlikely marriage, but everyone agreed it was a happy one. Further down the table, nearer to Philly, was the handsome African American, Brent Michaels, who was rumoured to be Lucy's ex-lover.

Then there was Philly. Only she was not Philly tonight. Her name was Cassandra. Lucy had shown no signs of recognising her, which was good. After all, it had been a long time since Lucy and Cassandra were at school together. They had been the best of friends, until Lucy stole Cassandra's boyfriend at the high school prom.

Lucy lifted the coffee cup to her lips, and as she did so, she gave Philly a strange look, almost as if she recognised her in that moment.

'No, it can't be . . . ' Lucy whispered. She drank her coffee. Suddenly her face contorted and she started to splutter. 'Poison,' she croaked. 'I've been . . . ' Her cup shattered on the parquet flooring, and Lucy slumped forward in her seat, her pretty face landing in what was left of her raspberry Pavlova.

'Oh my God, she's dead!' exclaimed Reg the vicar, leaping up and running to his wife's side.

'Golly gee, who could have done such a terrible thing?' said Brent Michaels.

'Oh, this is very exciting,' said Mrs Bennett, one of the other guests. 'Isn't it, Frank?' She nudged her husband who sat next to her.

'It's all right, I suppose. I thought there'd be more blood.' He looked like a man who had been cheated out of a special treat. 'What do we do now, then?'

'I suppose we get our notebooks out and start sleuthing,' said Mrs Bennett, practically slapping her lips together.

'Well if you ask me,' said Mr Graham, an elderly man in his seventies, 'it can't have been the husband. When they served the coffee, he'd popped off to the little boy's room.'

He sat around a small table in the drawing room with Mr and Mrs Bennett, as one of three teams racing to find out the identity of the murderer.

'Yes, but he might have slipped something into her cup as he walked past,' said Mrs Bennett. 'I think it was the ex-lover, Brent Michaels.' Her voice rose dramatically. 'Consumed by jealousy and thwarted in love, he decided that if he couldn't have her, no one else could. He's very handsome. Just like that nice Will Smith.' She sighed happily.

'Yes, but every time he went near to her, he sneezed,' said Frank Bennett. 'He was allergic to her perfume. So we'd have known if he touched her coffee, because he'd have had to lean over her.'

'Yes, but he might have taken an anti-wotsamine,' said Mrs Bennett as she scribbled down some notes.

'I'm not happy with this murder,' remarked Mr Graham. 'It's all a bit . . . I don't know . . . *dull*.'

'I said there should be more blood,' agreed Frank.

'And there are hardly any suspects,' said Mr Graham. 'Who have we got? That woman Cassandra . . . mind you, I don't like the look of her. Too pretty. They're the ones you've got to watch. Then there's the husband, Reg. What sort of name is that for a thirty-year-old vicar in this day and age? Then the ex-boyfriend, Brent Michaels. That's only three suspects.'

'There's the maid who let us in,' said Mrs Bennett. 'I haven't seen her since. Certainly not in the dining room.'

'Nah,' said Frank Bennett. 'She was played by the same one who's playing Cassandra. I recognised her pretty blue eyes.'

A woman from one of the other

5

tables called across. 'I just said there's not enough suspects. There should be at least half a dozen. Or a full dozen. Like Murder on the Orient Express.'

★　★　★

Philly listened from behind the door with a sinking feeling. Things were not going well for the second murder mystery weekend at Bedlington Hall.

'I said we needed more actors,' murmured Meg, who only half an hour earlier had thrilled everyone as Lucy the supermodel, choking to death on her coffee. If Mr Bennett was being picky, he might have suggested she was a bit short for a supermodel. However, she was taller than Philly and more slender, hence the part falling to her.

'I can't afford more actors, Meg. If you, Puck and Tony weren't doing it for free, I wouldn't be able to do this at all. I was hoping I'd make enough each time to add more. Plus . . . Oh, let's be honest, I'm not very good at writing them, am I? Mr Bennett's right. A thirty-year-old vicar called Reg just doesn't sound plausible nowadays. They're all called Blake or Brandon or something equally hip.'

'Something will work out,' said Puck. He had dropped his American accent. Whilst his real name was Mark Jenson, he had been known as Puck since he was five years old. Even his equity card listed him as Puck Jenson. 'So the script isn't perfect, but we can work on that. I don't think I should say 'golly gee' next time. That's a bit nineteen-fifties, don't you think? Like 'Hey, golly gee, let's put the show on right here, in the barn.''

'I'll be living in a barn if this doesn't work out,' rejoined Philly, glumly. 'And not one of those nice converted ones either. I'll have to tell the pigs to move over.'

'I'm sorry we didn't do better,' said Puck.

'Oh no, you did great.' Philly patted them both on the arm. 'So did Tony. Where is our portly vicar, by the way?'

'Gone to take his fat suit off for a bit,' said Meg. 'He said he was melting in it.'

'Oh, poor Tony,' said Philly. 'He really didn't have to go to all that trouble.'

'You know Tony,' said Puck. 'Doesn't matter if he's playing a jam doughnut in an advert or a portly vicar at a murder mystery weekend. He always likes to get into character.'

'They're all coming out,' said Meg, who had kept one eye on the drawing room door. 'I'd better go, considering I'm supposed to be dead.'

★ ★ ★

Three days later the guests had gone home, leaving Philly, Meg and Puck to clean up. Tony had left in the morning, having received a call from his agent offering him a spot in an annoying advert for car insurance.

'I can't believe he's the most successful amongst us,' said Puck, sighing. 'He never paid attention in drama school. Next thing you know he'll be playing English bad guys in American movies, whilst we'll be lucky if we get to be the back end of a pantomime horse.'

'I think that's what Tony's agent said he was playing in the ad,' said Philly, wiping the dishes. 'Look, thanks for helping me this weekend. I really couldn't have done it without you. I promise that as soon as I'm making a profit on this place, I'll pay you decent wages.'

'Hey, you feed us and let us sleep in a warm, dry bed,' said Meg, putting her arm around Philly's shoulders. 'That's payment enough. Especially since Puck's mum threw us out because we couldn't find jobs.'

'I've had an idea for the next murder mystery weekend if you can bear it,' said Philly. She hesitated when she saw her friends' pained expressions. 'Not that you have to do it. It's just that . . . well, you know that there are always adverts for Turkey and Tinsel weekends in the newspapers. They usually do them in early December.'

'Ye-es,' said Meg.

'Well, what about a Mistletoe Mystery weekend? We could write something with a Christmas theme. Maybe one of you could choke on the Christmas pudding or something.'

'I usually do when Meg makes it,' put in Puck.

Meg slapped him playfully with the dishcloth. 'Oy, behave or you'll be putting your own ready meals in the microwave, boyo.'

'Oh, I love it when you get all angry and Welsh,' said Puck, grinning back at her.

'Never mind,' said Philly, putting down the tea towel. 'I think I'm going to go and have a look in some of the rooms on the top floor. I haven't really had a chance since we moved in. I'm thinking there may be some nice furniture up there.'

'Hey, Philly,' said Puck. 'You know we've got your back, right? Whatever you want to do at Christmas, we're in.'

'I don't know what I'd do without friends like you,' she said, smiling. 'I promise that if this doesn't work, I'll think about selling the place.'

'You promised your godmother you wouldn't,' said Meg.

'I know, but I can't think of any other way to keep it. Unless I turn to crime, and I'd be useless at that.'

Philly left Meg and Puck chatting in the kitchen whilst she went around the house checking everything was back to normal. The good thing about paying guests was that they tended to take all their mess with them. Nevertheless, the house still took ages to clean up.

Her godmother, Robyn Sanderson, had died the year before, leaving Bedlington Hall in Midchester solely to Philly. Philly's father had been Robyn's second cousin and lawyer, helping to deal with problems on the Bedlington estate.

As Meg had reminded Philly, she had promised her godmother on her death-bed never to sell Bedlington Hall.

'I have given everything to that

house,' Robyn had said. 'It has been a demanding mistress. I'm leaving it to you, because I know you love it as much as I do. Don't sell it, Philly. No matter what you have to do, you must keep the house in the family.'

Philly, whose parents had died when she was little, had been raised by her godmother, at least for part of the time. Philly went to boarding school, and only saw her godmother in the holidays. Then when she left school and went to drama school, their lives had diverged even further. Every visit to Bedlington Hall had been magical. It was a house of various designs, a marriage of Tudor, Gothic, and Baroque, with each different part added by a new owner, creating a labyrinth of rooms.

For a short time, in the late 1940s and 50s, it had been a girl's boarding school. During the Second World War, the army had requisitioned it and turned it into a military hospital for recuperating soldiers. However, it had always been in the Sanderson family.

It had cost her godmother a fortune to install central heating and new bathrooms when she took the Hall back in the 1960s, yet even they were old and tired by the time Philly took charge of the house. The central heating banged loudly during the night, and due to the costs, it wasn't possible to heat every room. It might have added to the atmosphere during the murder mystery weekends, but it didn't always make living in the house very comfortable, especially with winter coming on.

Philly had taken out a business loan to update some of the bedrooms and add en-suite bathrooms for guests. Then she had been stung by many other costs associated with health and safety for anyone leasing rooms to the public. The loan was all gone, and she had barely broken even on the latest mystery weekend, due to so few people turning up. She had a small annuity left to her by her parents, but it wasn't enough to live on. It had merely helped keep a roof over her head before she was left the Hall. The annuity barely covered the upkeep of a large house, which devoured ten-pound notes at an alarming rate.

Philly wasn't afraid of hard work. Normally she supplemented her income and her 'resting' periods of acting by working as a waitress or cleaner. She had even worked in a factory, making boxes. Unfortunately the village of Midchester had only one restaurant, which was fully staffed. She had checked the newsagents' window for a card offering a cleaning post but to no avail, and there was no local industry to speak of. Midchester was the sort of place where people living in London had weekend cottages.

She was realistic enough to understand that even getting a full-time job wouldn't keep Bedlington Hall maintained. Unless she ever did get that big break in Hollywood, and that was unlikely to happen when she couldn't even afford the airfare to go over and meet film directors.

The main attic was locked and she hadn't yet found the key. She'd taken a large bunch of keys from the drawer in the kitchen, praying that one of them would fit. She rattled them as she walked along the passage, humming a song from Chicago.

'It'll be the last key,' she murmured to herself after the first ten didn't fit the lock. It was actually the last-but-one key on the ring. Philly breathed a sigh of relief when she felt the lock give.

The attic spanned the entire top floor of the house, and was full to the rafters with old furniture, suitcases, trunks, pictures and other debris from the house below. A dormer window was dirty and allowed very little light, and the ancient light bulb didn't cast much more illumination.

It would take her forever to search through it all, and she doubted any of it was worth much. She knew that when the house was turned into a hospital, then a boarding school, most of the larger family heirlooms had been put in storage elsewhere. She suspected that the things in the attic were worthless items that had just been put up out of the way when they were no longer needed.

She opened one of the trunks and found a load of clothes from the fifties. Another trunk contained clothing from an earlier era, and another had clothing dating back to Victorian times.

'Perfect,' she whispered. They would be ideal for the murder mystery weekends. So far they had had to borrow costumes from a friend in the BBC costume department, but they had been told under pain of death not to damage anything.

One trunk bore the name Dominique DuPont, but when Philly opened it, it only contained a painting.

The painting was about four feet high by three feet wide. Philly turned it over — hoping, but not really expecting, to find a masterpiece. At first she thought

16

it rather dull. It showed a tower set in front of a forest, and sitting upon the tower was a bird. Below the tower lay a long winding path, and walking along it was a small figure dressed in red.

The more she looked at it, the more she became transfixed by the colours, and the way the bird's eyes followed the small figure, yet also seemed to follow her whenever she moved away from the picture. There was something wrong with the perspective. The figure in red looked to be nearly half the height of the tower. She rubbed at the bottom with her finger. There were probably sounder, scientific ways of cleaning up a painting but she didn't have those at her disposal.

The name of the artist was Robespierre.

All Philly knew of Robespierre was that he was a rather unpleasant figure of the French Revolution. This painting couldn't be that old. It didn't even seem to be as old as the trunk in which it was stored. Something about the red outfit the figure wore was too modern looking. It looked like . . . an anorak.

★   ★   ★

'Robespierre,' mused Puck, as they ate a late supper of beans on toast in the drawing room. They all sat with trays on their knees, a bit fed up of the dining room, where most of the murderous action had taken place. 'I've heard of him. Used to run around with Andy Warhol's crowd in the sixties and seventies. Bit of a champagne socialist by all accounts.'

'The trunk it was stored in belonged to someone called Dominique DuPont,' Philly explained. 'But I think the trunk was older than the painting. A real forties or fifties style.'

'Now where have I heard that name before?' asked Meg. 'Dominique DuPont, I mean. Oh, I can't remember, but I'm sure it'll come to me.'

'She might have been a friend of my godmother,' said Philly. 'It sounds familiar to me, too. It's odd she left her trunk here.'

'You should take that picture to be valued,' said Puck. 'The Warhol connection should be worth something.'

'It could be worth millions,' said Meg excitedly. 'Then you'll have what you need to keep Bedlington Hall afloat, and Puck and I can get married . . . assuming you'd stump up for a wedding dress, that is.'

'Darling Meg,' said Philly, 'if this painting is worth just a fraction of that, I'll pay for the wedding and your honeymoon.'

As much as she would like to believe the painting would be worth a fortune, Philly didn't believe for one minute that her problems would be solved quite so easily.

2

Philly took the London road in her godmother's yellow Triumph Stag. The painting was wrapped securely in a sheet on the back seat.

Meg and Puck had waved her off that morning, wishing her luck, but it was fair to say that none of them really thought the painting would be worth anything.

'I feel resentful wasting the petrol money,' Philly had said. 'But if I don't try I might always regret it.'

She found the auction house first, then looked for somewhere to park. Though the painting was not huge, it was difficult to carry through the busy London streets. Her arms were aching by the time she finally reached the auction house door.

It was said to be one of the best in the country, so she hoped they'd be honest with her. She carried the painting up the steps, almost crashing into a man who was just coming out.

'I'm sorry,' she said. 'I was just . . . '

'No, it was my fault completely,' he said. He was about thirty years old with an American accent. He had the greyest eyes Philly had ever seen, and looked like the sort of White House intern they had in television dramas, clean-cut and handsome in a preppy way, but with a slightly tougher edge. Dressed in jeans, T-shirt and a tan leather jacket, he turned informal into an art form. She had to remind herself that tongue hanging out wasn't a good look for any woman.

'Wow, that's an interesting painting you have there.'

Philly looked down to see that the sheet had fallen off the Robespierre picture. 'Yes, I'm coming to get it valued. I'm hoping I'll at least get a Big Mac out of the proceeds.'

'Robespierre . . . ? Interesting.'

'You know him?'

'I know of him.'

'Oh well, that's hopeful. Do you work here at the auction house?' She couldn't think of anyone she would rather have answer her questions about the paintings.

'No, I just called in to see an old pal. My name is Matt Cassell, by the way.'

'Philly Sanderson.'

'Sanderson?'

'Yes. You know it?'

'No, no. Well, it was nice bumping into you, Philly.'

Ask him to go for coffee, her mind commanded.

'You too. Bye.' Damn! She would have to get better at asking men out. She smiled shyly and picked her painting up.

'Look . . . er . . . I know this is very forward,' said Matt, 'and I promise I don't do this sort of thing all the time. Would you like to go for a coffee? When you've had your painting valued?'

'Yes! Absolutely. I'd love to. I mean . . . thanks.' She wanted to kick herself for her over-enthusiasm. Her godmother had always said she should play it cool with men. The trouble was, that left men believing she was cool and unapproachable. She couldn't let this one go. 'I'll just deal with the painting first.'

'I'll come back in with you, if that's okay.'

'Thanks, I'd like that.'

'Great, because I'm afraid you'll fly away if I don't keep you in view.'

Philly had only reached the top of the steps when the doubts set in. Gorgeous men didn't just ask her out like that. Maybe he knew the painting was worth a fortune and had decided to latch on to her. On the other hand, he looked to be very much his own man. *How can you know that on five seconds' acquaintance?* she chided herself. He could be a murderer for all she knew.

On the other hand, he might seem perfectly nice but turn out to be one of those boyfriends from hell. The type who didn't like you going out with your friends, then turned out to be slowly poisoning you . . .

Philly tutted inwardly to herself. She really had appeared in too many bad television dramas!

The auction house reminded Philly of a library. The colours were muted, and the atmosphere matched. She was glad she had found a smart, 1950s-style grey suit in one of the trunks in the attic. It fitted her almost as if it were made for her. With her dark chestnut hair pinned back in a chignon, she hoped she looked sophisticated and business-like.

'If you were a blonde, Alfred Hitchcock would be swooning in his grave,' Meg had told her before she left.

There was a reception desk at the auctioneers, but no one staffed it. She tapped on a brass bell.

'Did you forget something, Matt?' a man shouted through.

'No, it's this young lady who's looking for you, Sebastian.'

Of course, thought Philly, *he had to*

be called Sebastian. He was a nice-looking young man, but appeared to have a bad smell under his nose, judging by how high he stuck it in the air when he looked at her. The suit wasn't going to impress him, that much was certain. He looked her up and down, disdainfully.

Unwittingly, Philly followed his gaze to her feet, and almost swore when she realised that she had forgotten to change out of her pink plimsolls, which she always used for driving. She had packed a pair of elegant black court shoes, but they were still in the boot of the car. To make matters worse, Matt's eyes had also followed Sebastian's to her feet.

She shuffled around a little, as if doing so would magically make the pink plimsolls disappear. It didn't work.

'I have this painting,' she said, putting it onto the reception desk with a bang. That took their attention from her feet! 'I wondered how to go about getting it valued. It's by Robespierre.

25

Two people I've spoken to have heard of him, so — '

'Everyone has heard of Robespierre,' said Sebastian, cutting her off abruptly. 'But I'm afraid your painting will not be worth anything other than as curiosity value.'

'Oh, why?'

'Robespierre was a master counterfeiter. I am guessing that's a copy of the Haywain that you have there.'

'No,' said Philly, feeling hot and bothered. 'It isn't actually. It's called The Robin Watches. I Googled it last night and it's not listed anywhere.'

She'd also done an Internet search for Robespierre, only to find over four million web pages about the French Revolution Robespierre rather than the artist. She gave up searching through them when she reached page ten of the listings and had read too many descriptions of people going to the guillotine.

'I'm sorry but you are wasting your time,' said Sebastian.

'Come on, Seb, give the girl a break,' said Matt. 'I'd like a closer look at the picture.'

A look passed between the two men, after which Sebastian was all smiles.

'Of course. It's possible that Robespierre did something original. I'm told he was very good in his youth, but he wanted to make a fast buck.'

'My friend said Robespierre was a champagne socialist,' said Philly.

'Yes, he was that too . . . oh, this is rather good . . . ' Sebastian seemed to have forgotten Matt and Philly were there. 'Very good indeed. I don't think I know it. Look, can you leave it here for a day or two and I'll find out what I can about it?'

'Erm . . . '

'It's perfectly okay. I'll give you a receipt for it, of course. Where did you find it exactly? It will help prove provenance.'

Philly quickly explained about inheriting Bedlington Hall from her godmother and finding the painting in the attic.

'There are more up there, but I haven't had time to check everything. I don't suppose it's worth it if Robespierre was a counterfeiter. Chances are they're all by him.'

'Don't be too hasty,' said Sebastian. 'You may have hit on something original, in which case it might be worth something.'

'Really? That's great.' Philly smiled. Okay, so it wasn't millions, but it might help her pay some of the costs of running the old house.

★ ★ ★

'So,' said Matt, sitting across from Philly in a coffee shop. 'What will I have seen you in?'

'I was a victim in *The Bill*. I had to utter the immortal lines, 'It was . . . it was . . . ugh' before dying.'

'*The Bill*?'

'Yes, it's a British cop drama. Then I was a road traffic victim in *Casualty*. Like *ER* but without George Clooney. I didn't have any lines in that before I was declared dead. I just had to lie there whilst they poked and prodded me. It's not easy to do when you're ticklish. That is probably why they've never asked me back, I suppose. Oh, and I was a cyberman . . . cyberperson . . . in *Doctor Who*.'

'Now *Doctor Who* I've heard of! Haven't you been in anything where you had a proper speaking role?'

'I was in a teen soap when I was about eighteen. I died in that too, of whatever disease was fashionable eight years ago. I've done a lot of stage work. Mostly small towns. I was Cinderella in Huddersfield last year, on the back of my work in the teen soap, but people only came to watch it because the baddie was being played by an ex-*Big Brother* contestant. What about you? What do you do?'

'I work for my dad's firm.'

'And what does your father's firm do?'

'We're in insurance. Kind of.'

Oh no, thought Philly, *he's the son of a mafia don*. They did a 'kind of' insurance. Like 'pay us all your money and we'll ensure we won't send Cousin Roberto around to break your legs'. She knew he was too handsome to be true.

'When you say 'kind of . . . ''

'It's mainly big stuff. Like paintings and sculptures.'

'Ah . . . ' Philly breathed a sigh of relief. 'So you couldn't promise me a reasonable quote on my car insurance whilst singing opera then?'

Matt laughed. 'You really don't want to hear me sing. Tell me about your godmother. How come she raised you?'

'Mum and dad died when I was seven.'

'I'm sorry, Philly.'

'It's all right. I've come to terms with it, I think. They'd gone on a second honeymoon, and were in a crash on the way home from the airport. So my godmother, Robyn, was made my guardian. She wasn't just my god-mother. We are related in some way.

Second cousin, something removed. I forget which. Dad was her second cousin, and her solicitor. I don't think she knew what to do with me, so she pretty much packed me off to boarding school within weeks of the funeral.'

'That must have been tough.'

'Yes . . . Yes, I suppose it was at the time. I had no other family to stay with. I was at boarding school for most of the year. Sometimes she'd come and take me out for the day during the break. Sometimes I'd go home with friends for the holidays. But for one fortnight a year, Aunt Robyn — I called her that even though she wasn't my aunt — would come and take me to Bedlington Hall to stay.'

'What did your aunt do? For a living, I mean?' Matt sipped his frothy coffee.

'She was a model. Though she was getting on a bit by the time I knew her. She used to model for Chanel in the fifties and sixties, and a few of the other big fashion houses. Beyond that, I don't think she did anything. When she retired she spent most of her life jetting around the world, staying with rich friends. Male friends mostly.' Philly grimaced, feeling a bit embarrassed talking about her godmother's love life to a complete stranger. 'She was always talking about Sheik This, and Prince That.'

'She sounds like quite a gal.'

'She was. Even though I didn't see her much, when I did, it was great fun. With Aunt Robyn there were no rules about bedtime or eating. Everything was geared towards enjoyment. She got me into acting. She had a great gift for mimicry, and she used to teach me all her tricks. It's a pity I'm not very good at it. We've been running murder mystery weekends at Bedlington Hall. My friends, Meg, Puck and I, that is.'

'Is Puck your boyfriend?'

'Oh no, he's Meg's fiancé. I went out on a couple of dates with him at drama school, then I introduced him to Meg and that was it. Fireworks, violins, you name it. All the clichés came together in their meeting.' *A bit like when I bumped into you,* she thought, but didn't say. She might have heard the fireworks and violins, but there was no reason he should have.

'And you're still her friend?' Matt raised an eyebrow.

'Of course. Meg is a wonderful friend. Besides Puck and I never had that spark and, like I said, we only went out on a couple of dates.'

In truth, Philly had been quite relieved. Puck and Meg's meeting gave her an excuse not to get too involved and risk getting her heart broken. In Philly's experience, people you loved were always taken away from you. 'Meg is a good friend,' Philly said defensively.

'I don't doubt it. She'd have to be to deserve a friend like you,' he added with a smile.

'Thank you.'

'So . . . there's no boyfriend around that I have to challenge to a duel?'

Philly laughed. 'Nope. Though I'd rather like to see that. It appeals to my sense of the dramatic. What about you? I bet you have an impossibly beautiful woman in your life.'

'Not until today.'

Philly's tummy did a triple back somersault. If he were too good to be true, would it hurt for her to enjoy being flattered by a handsome man? It had happened so rarely in her life. Certainly she had never met anyone like Matt before. 'Thank you,' she whispered, sipping her latte. 'That's a very kind thing to say.'

'I'm not being kind. I'm being honest. When I saw you outside the auction house . . . Oh, this is crazy, isn't it? Please tell me you heard the violins and fireworks too, Philly, or I'll think I'm going mad.'

'I heard them . . . '

'So when can I see you again?'

'Erm . . . I don't come down to London that often.'

'Then I'll come up to see you. Midchester, isn't it? Where exactly is that?'

'It's up in Shropshire. It's a lovely little village. It was a Roman garrison at one point, and we've the ruins to prove it. I could show them to you. If you're remotely interested.'

'I would love to see your Roman ruins. And Bedlington Hall. Is it haunted?'

'There was a rumour of a ghost haunting it at one point. The ghost of . . . oh, my goodness!'

'What?'

'Dominique DuPont. That's where I've heard that name!'

Matt frowned, looking puzzled.

'Sorry,' said Philly. 'When I found the painting, it was inside a large trunk. The label on the trunk said Dominique DuPont. I knew I'd heard it somewhere before. When Bedlington Hall was a school, a young student . . . a French girl . . . disappeared. I mean, completely disappeared. There were rumours that she haunted the school and the surrounding area for years afterwards. It was her trunk I found! I suppose the school must have put it in the attic when she left, hoping someone would eventually come for it.'

'Wow . . . now that is worth a visit. When can I come to see you, Philly?'

'Hmm,' she teased. 'Now I'm not so sure whether it's me you're interested in, or my ghost.'

'Can I be interested in both?'

'I suppose so.'

'Not to mention the Roman ruins. Midchester sounds like a crazy sort of place.'

'Really?' Philly giggled. 'Then you obviously don't get out much, Matt! It's pretty boring there most of the time.'

'I find that hard to believe,' said Matt, looking into her eyes.

'We're doing another murder mystery weekend at Christmas,' said Philly. 'Mistletoe Mystery. Perhaps you could come up for that?'

'That's weeks away. Do I have to wait that long?'

'I suppose you could come up this weekend . . . '

'Great. Are there any hotels in the area?'

'Oh, don't worry about that. There are loads of bedrooms in the Hall. I mean, if you wanted to stay there.'

'I thought you'd never ask.' Matt smiled.

Philly was shocked at her own forwardness. It would never have occurred to her to ask any other man to sleep in her home after such a short acquaintance. But with twenty bedrooms set aside for guests, it wasn't as if she was asking him to share her room. Not that the thought hadn't crossed her mind.

She knew she needed to put the brakes on a bit. Things were moving way too fast. Yet there was something inevitable about Matt and her feelings for him. As if they had always been there, but she hadn't known it. How did that song go? About knowing you loved someone before you met them? She hastily pushed that thought aside. She couldn't possibly love him.

She barely knew him. It was simply an overwhelming and rather exciting attraction. He was charming, handsome, and seemingly interested in her. Maybe all she really felt was gratitude.

★ ★ ★

It had started to rain when Matt walked her to her car. 'Can I give you a lift anywhere?' she asked him, unlocking her door.

'No, I'm good, thanks. So I'll come up to see you on Friday?'

'Yes. I'll look forward to it. You've got my number in case anything comes up.'

'I have. And you have mine, in case you decide to withdraw the invitation because you've decided I'm a raging psychopath.'

'Oh, I still haven't made up my mind on that,' said Philly.

In reply, Matt pulled her into his arms and kissed her. She clung to him, not wanting to let him go and lose this moment.

Her natural pessimism knew that it couldn't last. He would break the heart that she had protected for so long. But the sense of inevitability remained, and his kiss convinced her that she had embarked on a journey that she wouldn't stop until it reached the ultimate destination, no matter what it cost her.

When she walked through the door of Bedlington Hall late in the evening, Meg and Puck came running from the kitchen.

'I've had an idea for the Mistletoe Mystery weekend,' said Meg excitedly.

'I've got an idea to get the punters in,' said Puck.

'I've met someone drop-dead gorgeous,' said Philly.

Before Puck could open his mouth to speak, Meg clamped her hand across it. 'Philly goes first.'

3

'You mean you actually invited him to stay the weekend?' said Meg in amazement. They were sitting around the big kitchen table drinking coffee.

'Yes — you don't mind, do you?'

'Of course we don't mind,' said Puck. 'This is your house after all. It's just that you've never . . . I don't mean to be unkind, Philly, but you're not the most spontaneous person we've ever met. I seem to remember that when you and I dated, you had a schedule for the dates and we weren't allowed to deviate from it, no matter what.'

'Gosh, did I really? Oh yes, I remember now. But this feels right. Except it feels wrong, too. I know I'm going to get my heart broken, but I can't bear the thought of never seeing him again, whereas I think I was deliberately trying to scare you off because I didn't really fancy you. Sorry, Puck, no offence and all that.'

'Oh, don't worry, Philly, it's only my pride and masculinity you've destroyed.'

'Oy,' said Meg. 'I think you'll find that's my job nowadays.'

'And you're the only woman who could really do it,' said Puck, taking Meg's hand. Philly felt a pang of regret. Not for letting Puck go, but for never having known the love that Puck and Meg shared. She was wise enough to know that what she felt for Matt Cassell was probably nothing more than infatuation.

'So what about your ideas? Meg, you said something about the Mistletoe Mystery weekend.'

'Yes, I Googled that name, Dominique DuPont, and you'll never guess what?'

'She's a schoolgirl who went missing from Bedlington Hall when it was a boarding school.'

'Oh. Did you Google it too?'

'No, I remembered something about

41

it. I'm sure you've found out more.'

'Not much more. It happened in 1963. Dominique, who was seventeen at the time, simply upped and disappeared one day. The girl, her belongings, everything. There was a nationwide hunt, but they never found her. The odd thing is that when the school tried to contact her family to ask if she'd returned home, they'd disappeared too.'

'That is odd.'

'Yet children from the school were saying that they saw her in Midchester, or other places, for years after. A bit like Elvis packing groceries in a Texas supermarket, I suppose. So, I thought, what if we use that story for the Mistletoe Murder weekend? It was nearly fifty years ago, so anyone connected with it will probably be dead by now. It also cuts down on the number of people we'd have to use. Dominique could be played by one of us, then we could ditch her persona and be someone else. It should work as long as we made sure those two characters weren't in the room at the same time. We could come up with our own reason for her disappearance. I'm thinking international espionage.'

'In Midchester? It's hardly the place for spies.'

'But Bedlington Hall was a military hospital for a short time. What if one of the soldiers recuperating here had enemy plans for a secret weapon and had hidden them somewhere in the Hall, then died before he could hand them over? Dominique was a teenage spy, sent to search for them, but was popped off by the British government.'

'I should have let you write the plays before, Meg,' said Philly. 'Your plots are much more exciting than mine.'

'I'll be James Bond,' said Puck. He put his hand into the form of a gun. 'Licensed to thrill.'

'Ooh yes,' said Meg. 'Though you are much better-looking, darling, despite what Philly says.'

'I didn't say he wasn't good-looking. I just said I didn't fancy him, that's all.'

'And the knife twists again,' said Puck, theatrically pulling an imaginary dagger from his chest. 'I'm telling you, Philly, this Matt bloke had better be blooming fabulous. I shan't settle for being cast aside for anyone less than drop-dead gorgeous.'

'Yes, Puck, I dumped you years ago for a man I only met today. Though . . . '

'What?' Meg and Puck said in unison.

'Nothing. It's silly. I just had that feeling, when you meet someone and feel as if you've known them for eternity. Do you know what I mean?'

'We know,' said Meg, looking lovingly at her fiancé.

'What was your idea, Puck?' Philly asked.

'Oh yeah. I nearly forgot with all this romance in the air. You remember my sister, Rachel? She just got a job as a presenter for a local news station in this area. I phoned her this morning to ask if we could get a spot on one of the programmes. She's going to put it to her producers, but she thinks it's just the sort of thing they'll love, especially in the run-up to Christmas.'

'That's brilliant!'

'Rachel said,' Puck continued, 'that sometimes these things go national too, if it's considered interesting enough. So I reckon we should go looking in the attic, and get out some of the old stuff. Rachel said that the more antiques we can show the better, as it gives the place atmosphere.'

Philly clapped her hands together excitedly. 'This is so exciting. I don't know what I'd do without you two, honestly.'

★   ★   ★

Puck's sister phoned early the next morning to say that she would be coming at the weekend to film the house, so to have as many details of the mystery weekend as possible ready.

The three friends spent the next few days searching the attic for suitable furniture, paintings and ornaments. The 1970s orange and brown Dralon suite in the drawing room had been artfully covered in some chintz curtains to make them look more Victorian, and Puck had carried an old chaise longue down from the attic to add to the atmosphere.

They decorated the piano in the ballroom with old photographs of family, many of whom Philly didn't know.

Meg had thrown some patterned scarves, which she found in the trunks, over the standard lamps in every room to give each one a warm, comforting glow.

By the time they had finished, the downstairs rooms, such as the drawing room, sitting room and dining room, had a look of genteel clutter. They swept out the ballroom, and polished up the crystal chandeliers, hiring a polishing machine to make the wooden floor gleam. When they had finished, Puck took Meg in his arms and swung her around the ballroom.

'Ah,' said Philly, from the door, 'it's just like watching Beauty and the Beast.'

'Don't talk about the woman I love like that,' said Puck, earning himself a nudge in the ribs from Meg.

'It's a pity,' Philly said, as they all worked hard to get the rest of the house ready, 'that we couldn't have at least one room as a classroom. You know, for the story. I wonder why there are no old desks in the attic.'

'I suppose the people who ran the school took them with them when they left,' said Puck. 'Maybe we could hunt some down from a bargain sale, or something.'

'I don't think I can afford it. We'll just have to make do.'

'We could ask some of our friends who work behind the scenes in television,' Meg suggested. 'There must be loads of desks left over from *Grange Hill*.'

'There's no time to do it before the

weekend,' said Philly, 'but we'll look at that option before the guests arrive. It would be great, because we want the story to be realistic. I know what to do! We could have the guests as extra schoolchildren. Hunt down some old lesson plans from the fifties. There must be some online. There'd be some fun in that and it would fill in some of the plot, to give the story realism.'

'I agree!' said Meg. 'See, you are good at this.'

'The only trouble is,' said Puck, 'this was a girl's school. Might be difficult to know what to do with any male guests who come for the weekend.'

'Oh, we could gloss over that and make it unisex for the purposes of the story,' said Philly. 'It doesn't really matter too much, since we're making it all up anyway. But that does give me another idea. What if we involve the guests properly? Not just as visiting sleuths, but as people in the story. Once we know who's coming, we could write a part for them. They won't have to remember any lines. We'll just tell them who or what they're supposed to be and let them improvise. To keep it simple, and so we don't get confused, they can use their own names. We could even let one of them be the murderer, so that they all suspect each other. I bet they'd love that. And it'll help us get over the problem of not having enough actors.'

'Genius!' said Puck.

'Absolutely!' said Meg.

They thrashed out the details whilst they finished preparing the house. By the time Friday evening came they were exhausted, but happy.

* * *

Matt arrived just before dinner, driving a sleek black Mercedes, and looking every bit as handsome as Philly remembered. She had spent the week trying to convince herself that she wouldn't be as attracted to him on their second meeting. The flip her heart did on seeing him belied that notion.

'Okay,' said Meg, after the introductions were made. 'You were right, Philly. He's drop-dead gorgeous.'

Philly poked her in the ribs, whilst Matt smiled.

'What else has she been saying about me?'

'Oh,' said Puck, 'that you'll break her heart. But we're here to make sure that doesn't happen.'

'I have a feeling I should be very scared,' said Matt.

'You should,' said Puck. Philly got the impression that neither of her friends were joking.

'Right,' said Philly, 'can we stop the *Godfather* stuff now and just enjoy ourselves? Matt, you don't mind if we order food in, do you? We've been working hard all week.'

'That's fine by me.'

'Chinese?'

'Chinese is perfect. What have you all been up to?'

Philly told him about their plans as she showed him around the house. Meg and Puck had tactfully made themselves scarce.

'It should be all right,' she said, doubtfully. 'I mean this all happened about fifty years ago, so we shouldn't be hurting anyone, should we? Even if Dominique was still alive, she'd be in her mid to late sixties, so her parents would be long dead or at least extremely old.'

'Oh sure, yeah,' said Matt. 'It's strange, isn't it, that no one ever came forward?'

'Yes. It's almost as if she didn't exist. Except she did, because there are pictures of her online. She's a favourite on all those unsolved crime websites. There are all sorts of conspiracy theories. We're going with the spy angle.'

'A schoolgirl spy, hey? Sounds good. This house is great, Philly. No wonder you fight so hard to keep it.'

'I love it. It's the only home I've ever known. Or, at least, the only home I remember. I don't recall much about where I lived with Mum and Dad. I get the feeling we moved around a lot, as I have vague recollections of different houses and flats. I'll show you around outside tomorrow, if you want.'

'That would be great.'

'Oh, I forgot to tell you. There's a film crew coming. You don't have to be on telly if you don't want to, though.'

'I'd rather not be. Besides, this is your project.'

'Mine, Meg's and Puck's.'

'They seem like good people.'

'They are good people. They're my family now.'

They had arrived at the large drawing room. 'These pictures are interesting,' said Matt. 'Where did you get them from?' He pointed to a group of paintings of family scenes. They looked vaguely Dutch to Philly, although she didn't know where she got that impression.

'The attic. There's loads more up there.'

'Really? Are they originals?'

'I doubt it. I don't even recognise half the artists' names. Sadly there are no Van Goghs or Holbeins hanging about the place. I haven't heard back from your friend about the Robespierre painting yet.'

'These things take time,' said Matt. 'Don't worry, Sebastian's legit.'

'Oh, I'm sure he is. I wasn't suggesting . . . '

'No, I know you weren't, Philly.' He turned to face her, putting his hands on her shoulders. 'It's good to see you again.'

'You too . . . ' Her insides were turning to jelly.

Matt pulled her towards him and gave her a long, lingering kiss, which she found herself returning. 'Very, very good to see you,' he whispered. 'Today couldn't come quick enough for me.'

'I'm glad you're here.'

There was the sound of a car horn outside.

'That'll be the food,' she said, pulling away. He stopped her and, drawing her back into his arms, kissed her again.

Dinner was a lively affair. Matt seemed to very quickly pick up on the quirky sense of humour shared by the three friends, and joined in easily. It helped Philly to relax more. She had been eager for Meg and Puck to like him, and it seemed to her that they did.

'Philly says your family are in insurance,' said Puck. 'Expensive stuff.'

'That's right. Ships, yachts, works of art. You name it, we insure it. We even insured an athlete's legs for ten million bucks not long back.'

'Wow,' said Meg picking up on the last fact. 'That'd be some pay day if he ever trips over a paving stone, or something.'

Matt laughed. 'To get the full payout, the paving stone would have to remove his legs from his body.'

'There are streets just like that in some parts of Britain,' said Puck. Everyone laughed, and a conversation ensued where everyone had a story to tell about knowing someone who made a fortune for breaking a toenail on government property.

'So when are you having this Mistletoe Mystery weekend?' asked Matt.

'A couple of weeks before Christmas,' said Philly.

'Oh, that reminds me,' said Puck. 'Tony called while you were showing Matt around the house. He can't make it that weekend. He's got a proper gig on a television drama. So we don't have a headmaster.'

'Oh, no!' exclaimed Philly.

'A headmaster?' repeated Matt.

'Yes,' said Philly. 'Tony was going to play the part, but he was also going to be the master of ceremonies. You know, explaining to everyone what's what when they arrive. Can't you do it, Puck?'

'I'm cooking dinner on the first night, remember?'

'Oh yes. Puck is the only one amongst us who can really cook,' Philly explained to Matt.

'That's why I keep him around,' said Meg smiling. 'Pity, though. Tony was perfect. He has this really authoritarian voice, like Patrick Stewart as Jean-Luc Picard. Make it so,' she added in a deep voice.

'Could I do it?' said Matt. 'I don't sound like Patrick Stewart, but I did a bit of acting in school. I think I could manage to be a headmaster. And you Brits love an American accent, right?'

'Mmm,' said Meg, grinning. 'I think a lot of the female guests will gladly suspend disbelief when they see you, Matt.'

Puck frowned, but smiled widely when she blew him a placatory kiss.

'You . . . you'd really want to?' said Philly.

'Yeah, I'd love it. You guys make it sound like so much fun. Not that I want to push myself forward. I realise you hardly know me. But I'm yours if you want me. I promise I come really cheap. A Chinese meal and a kiss from

Philly will be payment enough.'

Philly hardly knew how to answer that.

'Just tell me what I have to do,' said Matt enthusiastically.

'It's simple really,' said Philly. 'There's no real script, just an outline. You greet the guests, then there's some health and safety stuff you need to do, then you explain the nature of the game. We can tell you all that before the day. As long as you get the basics right, you can improvise as much as you like.'

'But you can't be the murderer,' said Puck. 'We're saving that honour for one of the guests.'

'Damn,' said Matt with a grin. 'I really wanted to be an evil headmaster. I could have based him on the one at my school.'

'We can make you evil in some other way,' said Philly. 'Everyone will need at least one motive.'

The fine details of the weekend were thrashed out over coffee and fortune cookies.

Later, Philly showed Matt to his room.

'Where's your room?' he asked, when they reached his bedroom door.

'I don't think I'm ready to tell you that yet.'

'Things moving a little bit too quickly for you?'

'Yes, a little.'

'That's fine,' said Matt, pulling her into his arms and kissing her longingly again. 'I can wait. I had a great night tonight.'

'Yes — me too.' Philly had been delighted by how well he'd fitted in with her friends. It meant a lot to her that Meg and Puck liked him. 'If you're cold, there's an extra blanket in the wardrobe. This is a draughty old place this time of year.'

'I feel pretty warm at the moment,' murmured Matt, pulling her closer still.

'I won't be in the wardrobe,' Philly said, laughing.

'Pity.'

'Goodnight.' She managed to pull

herself away from his embrace, albeit reluctantly.

Later that night, when she was in bed, unable to sleep because her thoughts were full of Matt, Philly thought she heard footsteps on the floor above her.

There was no reason for anyone to go up there. None of the bedrooms was habitable. They were either empty or full of junk. She intended to renovate them at some point, when her finances improved.

She crept out of bed and put on her dressing gown, opening the door to the hallway. She didn't bother with the lights, as she had walked the hallway lots of times and her bedroom light cast a glow for part of the way. Tiptoeing to the junction of the stairs, Philly listened for any noise, but it had gone quiet. She decided she must have imagined it.

Turning, she screamed when she bumped into a solid, warm body. She recognised him by his cologne.

'Oh, Matt, you scared the life out of

me. What are you doing out here?'

'I went down for a drink of water and got lost on the way back to my bedroom. This place is like a maze. Sorry, I didn't mean to scare you.'

'That's okay.' Philly took a deep breath, trying to slow down her heart rate. 'Your room is that way.' She pointed to the right hand corridor. 'Second door on the left.'

'Oh yeah, easy when you know how. Goodnight.' He kissed her lightly on the lips.

She watched him walk back to his bedroom with a frown on her face.

Actually his bedroom was very easy to find. She had made sure of that when she chose it. Plus each room had a small hand basin with a clean glass, so a trip downstairs for water was not necessary.

Had Matt been creeping around upstairs? And if so, why?

4

Philly spent a sleepless night worrying about Matt. What had she been thinking, inviting a perfect stranger to stay in her house for the weekend? True, he was handsome and utterly charming, and he kissed like a dream, but what did she really know about him?

Her infatuation had got the better of her. Now she really did wonder if he were some sort of conman. All she knew about him was what he had told her.

At around two in the morning she got out of bed and fetched her laptop from the dressing table. She would do what all self-respecting paranoid people did in modern times. Google him.

A search for Matt Cassell turned up several Facebook pages, a couple of Twitter accounts, and finally a company called Cassell & Keep. True to his word, Matt was pictured on the company page as one of the directors. His father, who was a very handsome older version of Matt, was pictured above him. Perhaps, she thought, her imagination running riot as usual, he set up the webpage because he knew she would look for it. But there were also pictures of Matt and his father with celebrities and other high-profile clients, some dated several years earlier.

Unless the photographs had been mocked up, she doubted it was all thrown together in a few days. Unless he had a long-running swindle going and the website was part of that? But if that were the case, he was telling people how to find him.

The contact page gave the company address, and when Philly did a search for that, it was listed in several directories as genuinely belonging to Cassell & Keep.

Unless the people he conned were too ashamed to come forward. She had read about lonely women preyed upon by handsome young men, and divested of their cash and other belongings. But she had made it clear to Matt that she had no money. Perhaps he didn't believe her, because she owned Bedlington Hall. She had been approached by a few property developers, interested in buying up the land. It would have made her life much easier, but having promised her godmother never to sell, she had refused them all. Did Matt hope to seduce her into selling up?

There had to be more to it than that. He had latched on to her when she bumped into him on the steps of the auction house. When he had seen the Robespierre painting! Was that the reason? Could it be worth more than she thought? It was possible Matt thought there were other similar paintings in the house. She began to wonder if he and Sebastian were involved in some sort of scam, unknown to the respected auction house.

In the cold, early morning light as dawn broke, all of that seemed more possible than him being so instantly attracted to her. Such things didn't happen. At least, not to her. She knew she had been stupid to invite a man she barely knew to stay at the house, but at the time she had been so eager to see him again she forgot to be her usual, sensible self.

Now she wondered how to cool things. She couldn't be rude to him whilst he was staying, or just ask him to leave for no good reason — finding him on the stairs at night was hardly a hanging offence — but when the weekend was over, she wouldn't see him again. The thought pierced her heart like a dagger. She realised it would hurt more if he did turn out to be a conman after she had succumbed to his charms. Better to break her own heart than let him do it.

On the other hand, she did wonder if she were merely replaying her dates with Puck, and the way she deliberately sabotaged any chance of a relationship. The difference was that whilst she had liked Puck as a person, because he was handsome, funny and charming, there hadn't been the same connection she felt when she met Matt. With Matt there was a sense of inevitability, as if he'd been waiting in the wings all along, ready to make his entrance.

Philly often thought that fate sent her Puck so that Meg could be happy, and she liked that idea. She may fear a long-term relationship herself, but she loved seeing the two people she cared for most in the world happy together. What she had told Matt was true. They were her family, and the only people she could truly trust not to hurt her.

Perhaps, she thought idly, as she lay awake through to the dawn, she could introduce Matt to one of her other female friends. Puck's sister, for example. He would most certainly fancy Rachel Jenson. She was a very beautiful young woman and she was due to visit Bedlington Hall that very weekend. Yes — that might solve things.

So why did the thought of Matt

falling instantly in love with Puck's sister feel like a second dagger twisting in her heart?

The problem occupied her mind until she got out of bed, having given up any idea of sleeping, and crawled bleary-eyed down to the kitchen to prepare breakfast.

'Morning!' she said breezily when Matt arrived in the kitchen ten minutes later. 'Did you sleep well?' *Keep it calm and friendly, Philly*, she told herself. She fiddled with the coffee maker, suddenly forgetting how to use it.

'Yeah, great thanks. Once I got used to the unfamiliar sounds in the house.'

'Yes, it does rather moan and murmur at night, doesn't it? Would you like some coffee? Breakfast? I think we've got some real Shropshire bacon in the fridge. It's delicious. With some scrambled eggs, perhaps? And toast? Or would you just prefer cereal? Sit down and I'll sort something out.' She could hear her voice waffling on, trying hard to fill what would otherwise be an awkward silence.

'Could we start with a kiss?'

Philly hadn't realised how close to her he was. He spun her around and before she could argue, covered her mouth with his. She wanted to protest. To tell him that she was far too busy for that, but the warmth of his arms around her and the feel of his lips on hers forestalled any argument. Why was she thinking of sending him away when he made her feel this way? Oh no, what if he did fall in love with Rachel Jenson?

She pulled away rather abruptly.

'I have important things to do,' she said, forcing herself to sound far more light-hearted than she felt. 'And you're in my way, young man.'

'What's more important than kissing?'

'Right at this moment I can't think of anything, but I'm sure it will come to me,' she added trying to shrug off his embrace.

'Are you okay, Philly?' Matt stroked her cheek. He also kept his arms around her, neither of which did anything for her equilibrium. She reached out and held onto the worktop, as if suddenly adrift on a very choppy sea.

'Yes, of course, why?'

'I don't know. You seem a bit jumpy. Are you regretting inviting me down? Is that it? Because I could go and stay in a hotel. I know things have happened quickly . . .'

'No, please don't leave.' A few minutes before, she could have sworn she would be delighted if he just upped and left. Her need for him to stay hit her like a lightning bolt. 'I'm just . . . I'm not used to things happening this rapidly, and I need to get my breath back, that's all.' It was a pity he had just kissed it all away. 'Don't you know I'm Ms Organised? And you've thrown my schedule right out of the window.'

Matt smiled. 'What schedule was that? Get married at twenty-eight, have a baby at thirty?'

'Actually I was thinking of the

present. Prepare breakfast. Eat breakfast. Get the house ready for Rachel Jenson and the film crew. You're very distracting, you know.'

'I'm glad to hear it. The feeling is mutual, by the way.'

'Go and sit down and I'll bring your coffee. Do you want a bacon sandwich?'

'You don't have to do everything alone, you know? You make the coffee, I'll do the bacon and eggs.'

'No, I can't. You're a guest.'

'And you're going to wear yourself to a frazzle trying to get everything done. Where's the refrigerator?'

'It's that big white thing next to the door. And it's called a fridge here.'

'Really?' Matt grinned. 'No wonder I didn't recognise it. Make the coffee, woman, and let me do the breakfast. Will Puck and Meg want anything?'

'No, not yet. They tend to sleep in a bit at the weekend when we don't have guests.'

'So it's just you and me . . . '

'It seems like it.'

Matt went to the fridge and took out the bacon and eggs. 'How do you like your eggs? Over easy? Sunny side up?'

'I've no idea what any of that means,' said Philly. 'So just scramble them. When the coffee is done, I'll make toast.'

As they prepared breakfast, Philly had that feeling of inevitability again. They worked together well, and it felt as if they'd been eating breakfast together every day for years. Her anxieties of the night before began to disappear.

Any chance of being alone also disappeared. Within a few minutes of smelling the bacon frying, Meg and Puck appeared.

'That smells good,' said Puck.

'It certainly does,' said Meg.

'I'll throw in some more. As you can see, Philly has enslaved me already.'

'Oy! You offered. He offered,' she said to Puck, as she buttered the toast.

'Yeah, yeah, we know, Philly. Careful, Matt, she's a bit keen with that whip.'

'We still have the scars,' said Meg, pouring out a cup of steaming coffee.

'Did I mention I'd poisoned the coffee?' said Philly.

'What? Again?' Meg went into her best Lucy Crystal impression, pretending to choke after she sipped the coffee.

Breakfast turned out to be just as lively as dinner the night before. Once again Philly was impressed by just how easily Matt fitted in with her friends. With her life, in fact. He inhabited Bedlington Hall as if he were used to living in such a place. She supposed, if his family were rich, that he had an even more impressive house somewhere.

'I never though to ask, Matt. Do you live in Britain? Or America?' she asked, as they ate.

'A bit of both, depending on where the business needs me. I have an apartment at Canary Wharf, and another one in central New York.'

'Is that where you were born, Matt? You don't sound like a New Yorker.'

'You mean like Joe Pesci in *Good-fellas*? No, I was born in New England. My mom and dad still live there.'

'Ever been married?' asked Meg. Philly was surprised, but secretly glad. It was something she wondered, but was too afraid to ask.

'No, never married. I was engaged once, but it fell through.'

Philly couldn't help thinking that he made his engagement sound like a business deal.

'What happened?' she asked before she could stop herself.

'We just weren't suited.' Matt clamped his lips together, from which Philly got the idea that the conversation was well and truly over.

'Oh.' She drank down the last bit of coffee from her cup. 'Well, I suppose I ought to go and change out of my jim-jams and try to look presentable for the telly.'

'Yeah, good luck with that,' said Puck.

'What is it? Get-on-to-Philly Day?'

'Yep. Especially now there are three of us to gang up on you.'

'Hmm,' said Philly, with a wry grin. 'I do hope you all enjoy sleeping out in the stables tonight.'

'Oh please, Philly, not again,' said Meg mischievously, winking at Matt and Puck.

'I didn't realise you had stables,' said Matt. 'Do you have horses too?'

'No, I can't afford to keep them,' said Philly. 'In fact, I don't think there have been horses here since the Hall was a school.'

'I'd like to see them. In fact I'd like to see all the grounds. Maybe we could go for a walk after breakfast.'

* * *

It was a bright wintry morning, and the sky overhead was clear. Philly showed Matt around the grounds of Bedlington Hall as he requested. 'I haven't even had a chance to look all around the place since I inherited it,' she explained to him. 'I know I'm going to have to get a landscape gardener eventually, but that will have to wait.'

Parts of the garden were overgrown. There was a walled area, inside which were several greenhouses, but most of the glass had been smashed at some point. There were also what seemed to be vegetable plots in front of the greenhouses, but they too were overgrown.

'Maybe we could grow our own veg,' she said to Matt. 'It would cut down on costs.' He had been very quiet since they left the house. 'Matt?'

'Hmm?'

'I'm sorry if our questions seemed a bit intrusive. About your ex, I mean. It's just that we're used to telling each other everything and we forget sometimes that others have different barriers. We didn't mean to step over the mark.'

'You didn't. It's just a subject I hate talking about.'

'She must have hurt you badly.'

'Hey, it's a beautiful morning and

I'm with the most beautiful girl in the world. I don't need or want to think about the past.'

'Okay, I suppose that means I've done it again. Stepped over the mark, I mean.'

'You didn't. And you've every right to know about me. It's just that there are some things I'm not ready to share yet.' Matt took her hand in his.

'Fair enough. Let's go and look down near the lake. If I remember rightly, there are some old follies down there. Temples and things.'

'Things?'

'Yes, things! I don't know what you call them. I did buy a book on architecture, to try to work out how to describe Bedlington in brochures. I got confused just by all the different types of columns, though I think the ones in the hallway are ironic.'

'Ionic.'

'Yeah, whatever.'

'You really don't know much about art and architecture, do you?' Matt seemed strangely puzzled.

'Not a thing. Oh, I can tell a Da Vinci when I see one. Maybe even a pre-Raphaelite. But otherwise it's not really my subject. I suppose you know loads, working for the family business.'

'I know enough.'

Philly didn't know or understand why, but she sensed that once again Matt had closed the shutters on her.

The lake looked extraordinarily pretty with the winter sunshine upon it, surrounded by trees with a few remaining leaves glowing russet and yellow in the sunlight; a pre-Raphaelite landscape come to life. As Philly had promised, various follies were dotted around the bank of the lake. Arbours hidden away amongst the trees so that one could sit in the shade but still have a full view of the house and lake; small temples dedicated to various gods, mostly of the female variety, such as Aphrodite and Diana. They had walked several hundred yards when Philly stopped suddenly.

'It's the tower!' she said excitedly.

'The one from Robespierre's painting.'

Sure enough a stone tower, no more than seven feet in height, stood at the side of the lake with a path running from it to the water. Behind it wasn't the forest that Philly had seen in the picture, but a low hedge, with a gap in the centre.

Philly let go of Matt's hand and walked around the tower, looking for the right perspective. Finally she found it.

'The artist must have stood about here,' she said.

Matt went to stand next to her. 'Yeah, I guess he did.' He had that puzzled look on his face again. 'So I guess the painting does belong to this house.'

'What do you mean? Of course it belongs to this house. I found it in the attic.'

'Sorry,' said Matt, 'what I mean is that it was painted here, probably on commission. It wasn't bought from a gallery.'

Philly had the strong suspicion that it wasn't what he meant at all. She left him standing on the path and walked around to the back of the tower and found that it had an alcove with a stone seat built into it. Except that where all the other seats faced the lake, this one faced the Hall, looking through the gap in the hedge and across the lawns to the long Gothic façade of the house.

Inside the alcove, the walls were scratched with graffiti; mostly the names of girls whom Philly assumed had attended the school. One piece of graffiti was a heart and written inside was a time and partial date, leaving out the year. Philly assumed it was a secret assignation between one of the girls and a boy she shouldn't have been meeting. She scoured the walls and found there were several other hearts, all with a different time and date, usually a month or so apart. One heart was etched on the wall under the seat. She idly hoped that the young lovers had managed to run away together and get married.

Turning to look at the house, Philly had a fantasy of a teenage girl, running across those lawns to meet her boy-friend. That was when it occurred to her. What if that teenage girl had been Dominique DuPont? What if all she had done was run away with the boy she loved?

It didn't explain why her family also seemed to disappear, but they might have been ashamed if she'd run away with a lower class boy. Things were different in those days, and the lines between the classes were more pro-nounced.

What if, Philly thought, having gorged herself on too many Hollywood movies, the boy hadn't been a boy at all? He might have been an older man who could pass for a teenage boy. He might even have been a spy of some sort. There were many problems in France in the sixties, as Philly well knew from reading *The Day Of The Jackal*. The boy spy, an Algerian perhaps, might have killed the whole DuPont family — then it was all hushed up by the government.

She became so lost in her daydream, she almost forgot that she had left Matt alone. When she went back to him, he had moved nearer to the lake and had his back to her, looking into the distance. He was also talking into his mobile phone.

'No,' he was saying firmly, 'there's no need to send anyone else yet. I need to look around a bit more. I think the answer is in the attic, but it's locked . . . I'm sure I can get the key . . . No, no . . . Let me play this out my way, and then I'll be able to give you all you want.'

5

'You're very quiet,' said Matt, as they walked back up to the house. Philly had made sure that he didn't know she had overheard his telephone conversation by slipping back behind the small tower and waiting for him to come looking for her.

'I'm thinking,' she said rather shortly. It was something her godmother used to say when she was in one of her rare moods.

'Thinking about what? I hope it's not me, because I'm not sure I like the look on your face.'

Philly was not ready to tell him what she had heard. She wanted to find a way to catch him out properly. Then she could have him arrested for whatever it was he was up to. One thing of which she was certain, he wouldn't get the key to the attic, no matter how much he thought himself capable of seducing her. Not that there was anything in the attic worth bothering about — it was a matter of principle.

'There were loads of hearts with dates and time inside the small tower,' she said. 'I was thinking about the romance that led to them. I wondered if it had anything to do with Dominique DuPont.' There, that wasn't a lie. It was exactly what she had been thinking before she overheard the telephone conversation and realised that Matt was a sneak thief.

It all made sense now. His sudden attraction to her. She'd known all along it was too good to be true. No doubt he saw the Robespierre painting, heard about Bedlington Hall and decided she must be richer than she said.

'You think she ran off with this guy?'

'It did occur to me, yes, though that doesn't answer the question of why her family didn't come forward.' Philly hoped she sounded plausible and interested enough in Dominique's story. In reality, all she could think was that her heart was beginning to break, despite all her best efforts to protect it. Not that she would ever let him see that. If he knew how she really felt, then it would give him power over her, and she would not allow that to happen. 'Or perhaps,' she said, unable to stop the bitterness flowing from her lips, 'he thought she was rich and killed her when he found out she wasn't.'

She searched his face for a flicker of guilt, conscience, anything that might give him away. He looked just as gorgeous as ever, which didn't help her at all.

'Wow, that's a big jump from clandestine meetings in a folly at the side of a lake,' said Matt. 'What would he stand to gain from that? I mean, if they didn't marry first so that he inherited all her wealth? Surely a conman would just cut his losses and leave her heartbroken but alive.'

'Yes, that's a good point. Unless he

was really desperate. He might have owed money to someone, and pitched all his hopes on her.'

'Then if he'd any sense, he'd run like hell, without stopping to look behind him.'

'You don't know how desperate he was.'

'Nah, it doesn't make sense, Philly. I'm not saying that she didn't meet some guy who killed her, but it would have been a crime of passion. Or a suicide pact. Or maybe he was just a sicko. If he was a conman who found out she'd no money, then he would have switched his attentions to someone who did.'

'You sound as if you know a lot about it.'

'I've met a few conmen in my time, yes. They're not generally the passionate type. Oh sure, you get the odd one who has some other psychological problem, but mostly they're the type who don't waste time on cons that have come to nothing. They move on to the next one.' She couldn't help noticing that his voice became harder.

'So maybe he killed Dominique to stop her talking,' she said, pressing on regardless. 'Perhaps she found out about him and was going to blow the whistle.'

'I still think he'd have cut and run. If she was the only one who ever saw him, and if he used a false name, he could easily just disappear. After all, if she had nothing, then he couldn't be accused of taking anything from her. He wouldn't be the first guy to sweet-talk a girl. And if she was rich, his plan wouldn't have worked unless they married. Remember, she was only seventeen. She hadn't reached her majority so even if she had money in a Trust Fund, she wouldn't have had any access to it.'

'So perhaps she refused to marry him and then he became angry with her.'

'I guess that would work. I also guess you're only thinking your way through all of this for the sake of the crime on the mystery weekend, right?'

'Of course. Why else?'

But the more Philly thought about it, the more she thought she would like to find out what happened to Dominique DuPont. It seemed to her that the girl's fortunes were somehow tied up in her own. Or perhaps it was just a way of taking her mind off Matt and his deception.

She ought to order him out of the house immediately, after what she'd heard — but something stopped her. Maybe she was every bit as foolish as Dominique DuPont might have been, desperate to believe in a man who was clearly up to no good.

She had to admit there was a small part of her that hoped she had misunderstood Matt's telephone conversation. But she couldn't ignore the fact that he had told the person on the other end of the line about trying to get into the attic. Was it possible there was something up there that she didn't know about?

She was reminded of the film

Gaslight, in which Ingrid Bergman's psychotic husband, played by Charles Boyer, was desperate to find some precious jewels belonging to Ingrid's late aunt. They'd eventually been found sewn into a dress. Was there something like that in the attic of Bedlington Hall? More importantly, was Matt as psychotic as the man in the film? What lengths might he go to in order to find his heart's desire?

Looking at his clean-cut American good looks as they walked across the lawn, she found it hard to believe. Who knew what lay beneath the surface of his lightly tanned skin?

Ingrid Bergman's mistake in the film had been not trusting anyone with her fears. Philly was made of stronger stuff than that. As soon as she could, she would tell Meg and Puck what she had heard. There was safety in numbers.

Except . . . she was pretty sure that Puck would turn Matt straight out of the house, to protect Meg and Philly. That would be the right thing to do, of course. So why did she hesitate?

Philly's mind whirled. What could she do for the best? She should turn Matt out herself, yet something stopped her. Not only was Dominique DuPont's story tied up with hers somehow, she felt that Matt's story was too.

Everything from the moment they met had felt inevitable, including their meeting on the steps of the auction house. It really was as if he stepped onto the stage at exactly the right moment in Philly's life.

Yet it could be the wrong moment, if he meant her harm. Even a bad guy had to make his entrance sometime.

He was far too young to have known Dominique DuPont, but maybe he knew the man who conned her? Or maybe he knew the girl's family? Had Dominique left something in the attic at Bedlington Hall besides her trunk? Or perhaps, like the Robespierre painting, there was something else in the trunk. Philly made a silent promise to check it thoroughly as soon as she had a chance. It might have a secret compartment.

Meanwhile, her biggest question was whether to let Matt stay in the house for another night. He had offered to leave that morning and she kicked herself for not accepting the offer then.

As it turned out, she needn't have worried.

Rachel Jenson had already arrived with the film crew when Philly and Matt got to the house. She was in the kitchen with Puck and Meg, drinking coffee and eating chocolate brownies. Her cameraman, Joe, was with her. He looked as if he had eaten more than a few brownies in his time, but it didn't stop him tucking into the plateful that Meg put on the table.

'We just need some shots of the outside of the house, and then around the main rooms,' said Rachel. 'Then you can tell me all about your Mistletoe Mystery weekend.'

As she spoke, Matt received a message on his phone. 'Hey, I'm sorry,' he said to Philly. 'I have to leave.'

'Leave?'

'Yeah, yeah, my dad is ill. So I have to go to him. My mom needs me.'

Philly searched his face for signs of a lie. Either he was a very good actor, or he was genuinely distressed by the news.

'Of course you must go to him.'

'I promise I'll be back in time for the Mistletoe Mystery weekend. If I'm still welcome, that is.'

With a kitchen full of people, Philly couldn't say anything other than, 'Of course you're welcome. I . . . I hope your dad is okay.' She kissed him on the cheek hesitantly.

After he packed his things, she watched him drive away with a heavy heart. Had he realised she'd overheard his conversation and used the telephone message as an excuse to get away? His fears for his father, as he packed, had seemed real enough.

She noticed with an equally heavy heart that he didn't kiss her goodbye.

As he disappeared into the distance, she was half-afraid and half-hopeful that she would never see him again.

The rest of the day flew by. Philly, Puck and Meg's enthusiasm seemed to leap from them to Rachel and Joe, who did all they could to help sell the Mistletoe Mystery weekend.

'The item should go out on Monday evening,' explained Rachel as they saw her to the door. 'Only the local news, I'm afraid, but it's possible the national stations could pick it up. I don't want to be rude, but it depends if it's a slow news day.'

'I understand,' said Philly with a rueful smile.

'On the other hand,' said Rachel, 'the Dominique DuPont thing might help it along. I Googled her before I came here today and it's considered a big mystery amongst true crime buffs. So who knows?'

'Thanks, Rachel. And you, too, Joe. Your help really is appreciated. Perhaps you'd like to come and stay that weekend, if you're not busy? For free, of course.'

'You're not going to make money that way,' said Rachel, laughing. 'But maybe we could come and film some of it, as a follow-up story.'

'There must be brownies,' said Joe with a wink.

'There will be brownies,' promised Meg.

Puck kissed his sister goodbye, and when she and Joe had driven away, he clapped his hands together. 'I love it when a plan comes together,' he said, in the style of Hannibal from the *A-Team*. He became more serious. 'Pity about Matt's dad though. I hope he'll be all right.'

'Yes, me too,' said Philly soberly.

With Matt gone, she decided there was no reason at all to tell Puck and Meg about the telephone conversation by the lake. They would probably never see him again. Let them think he was a nice guy, and more importantly, let them go on believing that she hadn't just made an utter fool of herself over a conman.

*　*　*

The news report went out on the Monday, as promised. By Tuesday, the Dominique DuPont connection had earned it a few seconds on the main news. By Wednesday morning, Philly, Puck and Meg were inundated with telephone calls from people interested in attending the Mistletoe Mystery weekend. Within a few hours they had booked nearly every room.

It was late Wednesday evening when Philly received the most interesting call. It was from a well-spoken woman called Mrs Cunningham, who said she lived in Midchester.

'I would love to attend your Mistletoe Mystery weekend with my husband,' said Mrs Cunningham. 'He was the vicar in Midchester for many years, and we've done a bit of sleuthing in our time. But my own interest is personal. I was a teacher at Bedlington in the 1950s and 60s — and I knew Dominique DuPont myself.'

'Really? That's amazing,' breathed Philly. 'I wonder . . . well, since you're nearby, would it be an imposition for me to come and speak to you about her? It's not just for the story. I too have taken a personal interest in her.'

'Of course you may, dear. I'm not sure I can give you any clear answers, though.'

'That doesn't matter. Just speaking to someone who knew her would be so interesting.'

'Come down in the morning around eleven. I'll have the kettle on ready.'

True to her word, Mrs Cunningham was waiting in her trim bungalow on the edge of Midchester. She was a well-groomed, sprightly woman in her late seventies, who could easily have passed for someone ten or fifteen years younger. It was clear she had once been very pretty. Her greying hair showed hints of fiery red and her vivid green eyes were sharper than a pin.

She had tea and a plate of scones waiting in the tiny lounge, which was crammed with all manner of old furniture and books.

'We're still getting used to how small this place is,' she explained to Philly as she poured the tea. 'The vicarage was an old, rambling house. They let us live on in it for a while, since the new vicar bought a house amongst the new builds. Or they were new builds then. They must be twenty years old now. We moved here five years ago, and my first thought was, 'Where on earth are we going to put everything?' I still haven't answered my own question as you can see from the clutter. We're magpies, Andrew and I. That's my husband. Every year we decide we won't buy any more books, but then one trip to a second-hand book shop and we're back where we started.'

'I love books too,' Philly confessed. 'There's something truly magical about travelling to another world whilst sitting in your own armchair.'

Mrs Cunningham looked at her with approval. 'A person who doesn't love books doesn't love life, that's what I think.'

'I agree!'

'It wasn't always easy to impart that to the girls, though I hope I did my best. I imagine it's even harder for teachers nowadays, with television and the Internet to distract them. Not to mention those awful phones that ring wherever you are in the world. In my day if you missed a telephone call, people simply phoned you back. But now I sound like an old fogey, out of tune with society. We do have a computer . . . ' she glanced around the room. 'Somewhere amongst all the clutter. My grandson taught me how to send an email and how to . . . what do they call it? Surf? Now that's magical. Being able to surf when the nearest beach is miles away.' Mrs Cunningham winked.

Philly strongly suspected that her

hostess was nowhere near to being the vague old lady she pretended to be.

'But,' Mrs Cunningham continued, 'you're not here to talk about computing habits. You want to know about Dominique.'

'Yes, please. You said you knew her.'

Mrs Cunningham sighed. 'Yes, I did. Poor girl.'

'You say that as if you think she's dead.'

'There seems to be no other explanation. I told you, did I not, that my husband and I were amateur sleuths in our day? She was our only failure.' Mrs Cunningham's eyes became sad. 'But when I say 'poor girl', I don't mean it in that sense. I mean she was always a poor girl. She had a weight problem, and with her glasses and frizzy hair . . . well, she could have been pretty but she didn't make the most of herself. People think that young girls are only obsessed with image nowadays, but it isn't true. Anyone who looked different wasn't treated well. It didn't help that

Dominique wasn't the friendliest of creatures either. Also ... well, I shouldn't say this as it speaks ill of the dead, but she was very greedy.'

'Hence the weight problem?'

'Oh, I think it was more than just a problem. You see, she would receive these big trunks of food from her family. Now, the other girls always shared.' Mrs Cunningham smiled. 'Let's just say we turned a blind eye to midnight feasts ... but Dominique would not share. Once, a couple of the girls decided to steal her trunk, just for a laugh. They weren't dishonest and had no ideas of really stealing the food inside. But Dominique caught them and went absolutely crazy over it. She wanted them punished. She wanted them whipped. Well, whatever you might have heard of corporal punishment in schools in the 'old' days, we didn't cane our girls. They were punished with writing lines, of course. But it left Dominique more alone than ever. She wasn't a nice girl, and didn't invite friendships.'

'Yet you felt sorry for her . . . '

Mrs Cunningham nodded. 'Yes, I did. I know what it is to be different. My mother was a single parent at a time when such things were frowned upon. I used to try to talk to Dominique, and sometimes she would open up to me, mainly about the books she had read.'

'Did she ever talk of her family?'

'Only in very general terms. Her father, the Count, her mother, the Contessa. I rather think that they were virtual strangers to her. Many upper-class parents were like that back then. Palm a child off with a nanny, then straight off to boarding school. They seldom got to know their children.'

'But didn't her family disappear, too, at the same time as she did?'

'Yes, apparently.'

'Did they even exist?'

'Oh yes. Or at least, her father did. I met him when he brought her to the school the first time. A very handsome man as I remember rightly. Distinguished-looking. Everything you'd expect a French Count to be.' She sighed reflectively.

6

'Did they exist — I mean did the actual family exist? As French nobility, I mean,' Philly persisted.

'Do eat a scone, dear,' said Mrs Cunningham. 'Ah, yes, I see where you're going with it. There are many Counts in France, of course, and many of them very minor nobility. Plus, a lot call themselves 'Count' for no reason, or because, as in England, they've bought a title which means absolutely nothing in terms of nobility. It turned out their name did fit with one branch of the nobility, but it couldn't be proved one way or another. If her father was an impostor, it had been well-planned. But it makes little sense why they would do such a thing. Bedlington Hall, though a wonderful school in my eyes, was not considered one of the top girls' schools. Most of our girls came from the nouveau riche. Not a princess or a titled lady amongst them.'

'Tell me about the time Dominique disappeared,' said Philly, biting into a buttered scone. 'This is delicious,' she added. 'You must give my friend, Puck, the recipe.'

Mrs Cunningham laughed. 'Puck? Is he as mischievous as the Shakespeare character?'

'Oh, yes. But he's very nice too. So is my friend, Meg. They're going to get married.'

'Ah, so he's not the young man in your life then?'

'No, I don't have a young man in my life,' said Philly, almost choking on the scone.

'Really? I could have sworn . . . Never mind. There isn't much to tell about the time Dominique disappeared. One day she was there, the next day she had gone. Literally vanished. No one saw her leave, though some of the girls insisted they saw her in Midchester once. They built up some story of how she had fallen in love with a local boy and . . . '

'That's what I thought!' Philly put her plate down. 'Do you remember the small tower next to the lake? With the seat facing the house?'

'Yes, of course.'

'There were hearts in there, with dates and times. I wondered if Dominique had met someone there.'

'I hardly think so, dear. As you pointed out, the tower faces the house, and it can be seen from the house. Surely it would have been better to meet in one of the other follies, which faced the lake?'

'Yes, I suppose so.' Philly felt deflated, as if an avenue had closed to her. 'I wondered if she'd been meeting a young man and either run away with him or . . . ' She left the rest unsaid.

Mrs Cunningham nodded. 'Of course that thought crossed all our minds, but I can't see it. As I've said, Dominique was — I'm sorry to be cruel — without graces.'

'But that wouldn't matter if he thought there might be money at the end of it.'

'I suppose so, but there were girls with much richer fathers. I had the impression from Dominique that her family lived in genteel poverty. Even paying for her to attend Bedlington Hall was a stretch for their finances. I'm sure any young man taking an interest would have soon found that out. No, Dominique's story has some other truth behind it that we haven't found. People don't just disappear, taking all their luggage and belongings with them . . .'

'But she didn't take her luggage. She left one trunk. I found it in the attic. It had her name on it.'

'The attic?' Mrs Cunningham frowned. 'That's very strange.'

'Why?'

'You know, of course, that we rented Bedlington Hall from the owners, your relatives the Sandersons. They lived abroad and had done so since before the Second World War. I gather they weren't very well off and it was cheaper to rent the Hall to us and live overseas. But we only had access to the lower rooms and the first two floors. The Sandersons had put all their own belongings in the attic and it was kept locked. We didn't even have the key, and the girls were forbidden to go up to that floor. In fact, I don't know if it's still there, but there was once a locked door at the bottom of the staircase, to ensure no one entered. Some of the girls used to try to go up to that landing to smoke, you see.'

'That is strange. Unless one of the Sandersons found the trunk afterwards and put it in the attic.'

'We all combed those grounds thoroughly,' said Mrs Cunningham. 'The staff, the police, even the girls. If that trunk was anywhere to be found, we would have found it. To all intents and purposes, Dominique left with everything she owned, which is what made her disappearing act so amazing.

So how the trunk got into the attic, I don't know.'

'Was there anyone who had a key to the attic? A janitor or caretaker, pehaps?'

'I don't think so, dear.' Mrs Cunningham shook her head. 'It's possible someone did, in case of fire. Though with it being the top floor, that wouldn't have been an issue. No one went up there. Of course, my memory may not be what it was.'

Philly had the feeling that Mrs Cunningham's memory was as perfect sitting in the tiny bungalow as it had been nearly fifty years before when she was a teacher at Bedlington Hall.

The front door slammed shut, making Philly jump.

'Don't worry, that will be my husband. Is that you, Drew?'

'It certainly is. Do I smell scones?'

An elderly man with a ramrod-straight back entered the room. Like his wife, he had a twinkle in his eyes. Philly suspected that fifty years ago he had made female parishioners' hearts flutter. It was clear from the way they looked at each other that he still made his wife's heart flutter — and vice versa.

'Drew, this is Philly Sanderson, from up at Bedlington Hall.'

'Sanderson? Now there's a name to be reckoned with. I'm very pleased to meet you, Miss Sanderson. Or should I call you Ms nowadays?' said Reverend Cunningham, holding out his hand. 'We never got to meet your godmother, and were afraid you would be another one not to show your face in Midchester. She kept herself to herself rather.'

'I'm very glad I have,' said Philly, shaking the Reverend's hand and smiling. 'I hope I shall see you both more often.' As she said it, she knew it was true. She liked the elderly couple who had fancied themselves as sleuths once upon a time. 'Perhaps you can tell me more about Midchester's history. I'm afraid my own knowledge is very scant.'

Philly stayed a while longer talking to

them. As well as filling her in on the history of the area, most of it of the criminal variety, they discussed Dominique DuPont for quite a while. The story always came back to the same point. The girl had just disappeared, leaving no trace that she ever existed.

'I meant to ask,' said Philly as she was leaving, 'whether you'd heard of a painter called Robespierre.'

'Yes. A bit of a naughty boy, by all accounts,' the Reverend replied. 'He was from this area. Not that we knew him. He says he was born in poverty, then he became a bit of a champagne socialist, always railing against the system that kept him and others in chains, whilst living it up in the South of France, or knocking around New York with Warhol and his cronies. I don't think Robespierre let those chains hold him down that much. He got into trouble a while ago for art forgery but managed to take off to a country without an extradition treaty.'

It was pretty much what Philly and Meg had found out on the Internet. 'Robespierre seems to have disappeared,' she told the Cunninghams. 'I've been trying to track him down. I found one of his paintings in Dominique's trunk. But I'm pretty sure it was from a later time.'

'I was just about to say that it couldn't have been whilst Dominique was at the school,' said Mrs Cunningham. 'He wouldn't have been that old. Of course, he may have started painting young.'

'Do you recall ever seeing any young men around the school?' asked Philly.

'Dozens of them, dear,' said Mrs Cunningham with a smile. 'Our girls weren't in a convent, you know, and whilst we tried to stop them forming . . . shall we say, unpalatable relationships . . . we couldn't stop them being interested in boys. Some young men used to come up from the village and escort the girls to local dances. There was always a teacher to supervise, but I won't pretend that the older girls didn't find inventive ways to lose that teacher sometimes.'

'But you don't think Dominique was attached to anyone in particular?' Philly asked.

'No. I'd say she wasn't interested in boys at all, so didn't give out what the youth of today call 'vibes'. Do you see how good I am with modern language?' Mrs Cunningham added, her eyes twinkling in her husband's direction.

$\star$ $\star$ $\star$

There had to be a rational explanation as to why the trunk and picture were in the attic, Philly thought as she walked back to Bedlington Hall. Mrs Cunningham had promised she would try to remember the name of the caretaker who used to work at the school. Chances are, if there had been one, he or she might be dead by now as the role tended to go to an older person.

It occurred to Philly that there might

be some students who knew Dominique. If they were aged eleven to
eighteen in the sixties, they would only
be in their early to mid sixties now. Yet
Mrs Cunningham had made it clear
that Dominique wasn't attached to any
of the girls at the school. In fact, there
seemed to have been quite a lot of
animosity between her and the other
young students.

Philly had known girls just like
Dominique at her own school. They
alienated everyone by being snappy and
unpleasant. It was not always clear
whose fault it was; the girl for not
trying hard enough to fit in, or the
other children for not accepting that
people were different. Not everyone
could be a natural beauty or charm the
birds out of the trees. On the other
hand, friendship was a two-way street,
and one only got out of it what one put
in.

She had once tried making friends
with one of the girls, more out of pity
than anything, but had found it

draining to deal with her new friend's moods, which blew hot and cold depending on the day of the week. In the end, Philly had stopped hanging around with her, for which she was blamed in a horrid and humiliating row in the school playground soon afterwards. She had not been articulate enough at the time to explain that it was her friend's sullen behaviour that had pushed her away, and to this day she felt guilty that she didn't try harder to cement the friendship. It was a relief when the girl was taken out of that school and sent to a different one. Only then did Philly and her other friends learn that it was the latest in a long line of schools where the sullen girl had failed to fit in.

Perhaps that was the simple answer to Dominique's disappearance. Perhaps her parents had taken her from that school and sent her to another one, but been too embarrassed to admit to the teachers at Bedlington Hall that their difficult daughter had once again outstayed her welcome.

The more she thought about it, the more that answer didn't make sense. The family would surely not have let the mythology surrounding Dominique's disappearance continue. Unless they had some other reason for not coming forward. Perhaps the mysterious but handsome father had caused his daughter's demise. Her head spun, and she knew she was probably over-thinking it all. What did it matter anyway? It was a fifty-year-old mystery, after all.

Once again, Philly was convinced that somehow finding out what happened to Dominique was tied up with her own life. Why, she didn't know. But a girl had gone missing from the house that Philly now owned, and it seemed that it was her responsibility to find out what happened. She wished her godmother was still alive. Robyn Sanderson would know everything about the history of Bedlington Hall. There might be some clues there.

If Philly was being honest, she knew that the only reason she had fixated on Dominique was to get Matt out of her mind.

She had hoped that when he left, her feelings for him would fade, especially since it was clear he had intended to steal from her. Instead she found him haunting her dreams.

'I will not make a fool of myself,' she whispered as she approached Bedlington Hall.

Almost as if thinking about him set the spell going again, when she entered the hallway, Puck came from the kitchen. 'There you are,' he said. 'Matt phoned. He says he's been trying to ring your mobile.'

'Oh, I must have forgotten to take it with me,' Philly lied. She had left it behind intentionally, half-afraid that Matt would call and churn her up again.

'He says to tell you that his dad's okay.'

Philly felt a momentary pang of guilt.

She really ought to have called Matt to ask after his father. The trouble was, she'd no way of knowing if he'd told the truth. She supposed even a conman's father took ill sometimes, and he had looked genuinely concerned when he left. But that might have been because he realised the game was up.

'Oh, that's good,' she said, absent-mindedly. She started to climb the stairs, determined to search the attic. Since Matt had mentioned looking for the key, she'd kept it with her at all times.

'Phil?' Puck stood at the bottom of the stairs, leaning on the banister. Philly wished he wouldn't do it as the banister rocked slightly, reminding her of even more repairs needed in the big, old house.

'Yeah?' She turned around to look at him.

'Did something happen with you and Matt?'

'No, nothing.'

'Are you sure? Because a few days

ago you thought he was the best thing since sliced bread and now you look all worried when I mention his name. If he's hurt you . . . '

'It's all right, Sir Galahad,' Philly answered, smiling. 'I don't need you to defend my honour.'

'You do know that in films, when someone keeps things from their friends, bad things always happen.'

'We're not in a film, Puck.'

'No, but I still think you should tell us.'

Philly sat down on the stairs. As if realising she had a story to tell, Puck took a few steps upwards and sat just below her. 'Go on, what did he do?'

She explained about the telephone call she'd overheard.

'So you think he's a conman?' Puck asked thoughtfully.

'Why else would he want to go into the attic?'

'Did you see any jewel-encrusted dresses whilst you were up there?'

Philly laughed. '*Gaslight* was my first

116

thought too. No, but I haven't finished searching yet. That's what I'm going to do now.'

'Meg and I will help you. If there's any jewels to be had, I reckon we deserve them. I mean, you deserve them, of course.'

'You know I'd share.'

'I know you would, petal, but you don't have to. But what are we going to do about Matt?'

'Perhaps we should stop him coming to the Mistletoe Mystery weekend,' Philly suggested with a heavy heart.

'Or perhaps we should lay a trap for the evil so-and-so, then hand him over to the police.'

'Puck, that won't be necessary, will it?'

'Listen to yourself. You're actually trying to protect him.'

'No, that's not it,' said Philly, hotly, with a blush rising in her cheeks. 'I just thought of how embarrassing it would be if everyone knew I'd been taken in.'

'But you haven't been. You found out

before it was too late. I'm proud of you.'

'Me too,' said Meg, coming around the bottom of the staircase. 'And yes, I've been eavesdropping outrageously. It's such a fascinating thing to do. Puck is right. We should set a trap for Matt. Maybe when he comes here, we could mention there are jewels hidden somewhere in the house.'

'It seems he already knows that!' said Philly.

'Or maybe he only suspects it at the moment,' said Meg. 'It could be one of those myths that go around the criminal fraternity. Meanwhile, we'll hunt for the real treasure and get it put somewhere safe before anyone else can steal it. Oh, this is going to be fun! The three amigos, fighting crime.'

'You know that the three amigos in the film were a bunch of idiots, right?' said Philly.

'Yes, but they were also a bunch of actors who eventually won the day,' said Puck. 'That's if you can do this, Philly.'

'Of course I can do it.'

'Are you sure?' asked Meg. 'It's clear you've still got the hots for him.'

'But now I know he's a conman, I'm sure I'll get over it. In fact, I already am. You're right, we should hand him over to the police. He's obviously not a very likeable person really and now the scales have fallen from my eyes, I'll be fine.'

'Hmm,' said Meg.

'Hmm,' said Puck.

Philly guessed from their response that she hadn't convinced her friends any more than she had convinced herself.

7

'Ladies and gentlemen, welcome to Bedlington Hall.' Matt stood halfway up the stairs, looking very impressive in his tweed headmaster's suit, with leather elbow pads. A little young for the role perhaps, but judging by the looks on the faces of the women in the crowd, that didn't matter. His good looks and American accent gave him a Hollywood glamour that the females clearly found very attractive.

Philly watched him as he held the guests in the palm of his hand. 'This weekend,' Matt continued, 'we are taking you back to the time when Bedlington Hall was a boarding school and together we will investigate the disappearance of Dominique DuPont. But first, a few health and safety rules. Boring, I know, but necessary.' Matt quickly went through what to do in the event of a fire, going into air steward mode, moving his arms accordingly. 'The exits are here, here and here, and please don't forget your whistles. They'll be very important if we lose you in the snow.' This was followed by general laughter.

It had indeed started snowing the day before, giving the house a real festive feel, with its open fires and Christmas trimmings. The banging radiators in the ancient central heating system weren't so wonderful, but Philly had been assured by Mrs Cunningham that it was quite authentic.

'The system we had always banged something dreadful, dear,' the vicar's wife had said. 'It's all part of the charm, and really takes me back.'

'Now let's get on to the entertainment,' Matt continued. 'The main drama will only take place in the designated downstairs rooms. I gather you all have your itineraries?' He looked around at a silent chorus of nods. 'Yes, that's great. They will show where and when you can expect to see the next part of the story. When you move up these stairs into your own bedrooms, you are offstage, as we say in the theatre. So whatever role you have been assigned should only be played downstairs. In your bedrooms you'll have privacy and space to be yourselves again. So I hope it goes without saying that no one is to barge into anyone else's room looking for clues.

'The kitchen is also off limits for clue hunting, and therefore is also considered offstage. We're back to good old health and safety again. All clues are either in the main downstairs rooms, as stated on the itinerary, or in the gardens nearest to the Hall. I can promise you that because of the snow, very few clues are outside. We do ask that you leave all clues exactly where you find them, so that others can find them too. If you have a camera, you're welcome to take pictures. I bet you're all dying to get into your roles, so without further ado . . . '

'I'm afraid I won't be able to stay in character at all,' said Mrs Bennett, who despite her misgivings during the last weekend had returned with her husband. Their friend and fellow sleuth, Mr Graham, had also returned, much to Philly's surprise.

'Don't worry.' Matt flashed a stunning smile. 'We don't expect you all to be word perfect all the time and we understand that some of you may feel nervous or silly. I mentioned that the kitchen was offstage. It is, but as a way of helping you get to know each other, we will split you into separate groups. Tonight dinner is prepared by our chef, Puck Jenson, and there will be a continental breakfast buffet in the mornings. But for lunch and dinner we are going to let you all loose in the kitchen in your designated groups. Now don't look so alarmed. All ingredients and recipes are set out for you and one of the staff will be on hand to help you along.'

'I didn't think I'd have to cook my

own dinner,' said Mr Bennett grumpily.

'It was mentioned in the brochure,' said Matt, airily. 'Come on, it'll be fun. You can discuss the case with each other as the groups you're put in to prepare meals will be the same groups you're in to solve the crime.'

Philly almost reminded him there hadn't been a brochure for the weekend. There hadn't been time or money to create anything other than a small flyer. On seeing that everyone else accepted what he said without question, she held her tongue. He was certainly convincing. It was something she would have to remind herself about whenever she thought of succumbing to his obvious charms.

'Now,' said Matt, clapping his hands together. 'I'm going to be handing out your roles. They are non-gender specific and you'll keep your own names, so as not to confuse anyone. Some of you may be teachers, others schoolchildren . . . for the purposes of this weekend, the school which was a girl's school will also welcome boys . . . erm . . . ' He read from his notes. 'There are janitors, school nurses or doctors. You won't know what you are until you get your slip of paper and the great thing is that we don't know what you are either. You make up the character as you go along. And because this is a mystery, we want you all to be plausible suspects. So you can each come up with your own motive for being behind the disappearance of Dominique DuPont. Er . . . let's keep it clean though, hey, folks? Remember that Dominique, though over the British age of consent, was still a schoolgirl, so we don't really want any nasty business.'

'Is one of us going to be the murderer?' asked Mrs Cunningham, her sharp eyes twinkling.

'Well, who knows?' Matt winked at her. 'That's for you to work out.'

'I wonder,' said Mrs Cunningham, 'if I may be cheeky and ask if I can play the person I really was at the time. I was the English teacher at Bedlington Hall.'

Everyone looked towards Mrs Cunningham with interest. Philly got the distinct feeling the vicar's wife had just become a real suspect in their eyes. Mrs Cunningham either didn't notice or chose not to worry about it.

Matt glanced across to Philly who nodded back. 'Sure,' he said to Mrs Cunningham. 'If that's what you'd prefer.'

'Can I play the RE teacher who is hopelessly in love with the English teacher?' asked Reverend Cunningham to a chorus of 'awws' from the guests. 'Just joking. I'm happy to go along with whatever the card says. Either way I'll be hopelessly in love with the English teacher.'

'I can see why, Reverend,' said Matt.

'Ooh, you young charmer!' Mrs Cunningham laughed. 'Careful, Drew, he'll be stealing me from you.'

'Then they'll be investigating the disappearance of Mr Cassell,' said the vicar, light-heartedly.

'Can we get on?' said a sharp voice from the crowd. Everyone turned to see an elderly man wearing a flat cap.

'You're Mr Scattergood, right?' said Matt.

'That's right, Stan Scattergood, and I'd really like to get my dinner,' he added.

'But we're just getting to know each other,' another man replied. He spoke with an attractive French accent. He was probably in his late sixties, yet could easily pass for someone younger. He looked very suave and sophisticated, reminding Philly of Sasha Distel.

'As you say, Monsieur,' said Matt, 'we're just getting to know each other here.'

The Frenchman bowed. 'I am Armand De Lacey.' Philly vaguely remembered the name from the list of guests.

'Oh, that's just what we need,' said Mrs Cunningham with a smile. 'A charming French master.'

Monsieur De Lacey smiled back at

Mrs Cunningham and bowed again. 'Madame, I am the one who is charmed.'

It seemed to Philly that Matt had a sudden rival for the female affections as all the women's heads had turned to look at Monsieur De Lacey. Despite his age, he had no shortage of admirers. He was the sort of man who retained his appeal, regardless of age, like Sean Connery.

Stan Scattergood folded his arms and harrumphed. No one was looking at him.

'Don't worry, mate,' said Frank Bennett. 'I'm like you. I just want my dinner. I only come on these things because the wife drags me out.'

'Ooh, you liar,' said Mrs Bennett. 'I wanted to go to Majorca for a week, but you said this was a much cheaper option.'

'Well . . . ' Matt raised a hand. 'I think it's about time we let you go to your rooms and unpack. Dinner will be served at seven thirty, but there are tea-making facilities in your rooms so you'll just have time to get what you English call a nice cuppa. As you pass me on the stairs, I'll hand you your roles.'

Matt walked to the bottom step, and did just that as everyone filed past.

When they had all gone he looked at Philly and said, 'Well, how did I do?'

'You did great. Really.'

'You sound surprised.'

'No, I'm not surprised at all. I knew you could charm the birds off the trees.'

'Yet I don't seem to be having that effect on you at the moment, Philly.'

'It's just as I said when you arrived — I need things to slow down a bit, that's all.'

'I understand that. What I don't understand is why you've done your best to avoid me.'

'I haven't avoided you. I've been really busy, getting everything ready.' It was half the truth, except that she had used being busy as an excuse.

In the weeks leading up to the

weekend, Philly, Puck and Meg had spent every waking hour going through the attic, trying to find out what was in there that fascinated Matt. There had been more pictures, but they were tiny in comparison to Robespierre's painting of the tower. They were mostly of Madonnas and the baby Jesus. The friends guessed that they were not worth much, as they were merely smaller copies of the original Old Masters.

Puck had suggested putting them along the hallways. 'Seeing as it's Christmas,' he said. 'Baby Jesus and all that.'

Philly had been reluctant. 'Until we know what Matt's looking for, I think we should leave everything locked away up here. For all we know, we could put the very thing he wants on show. Then he could just walk out with whatever it is whilst we're not looking. Our best chance of catching him is if he goes up to the attic.'

They had arranged to set a trap,

leaving the key where Matt could find it. Philly had even separated it from all the others, and put a label marked 'attic' on it. With everything else they needed to do that weekend, looking after guests and going through the pantomime of Dominique's story, it would be a wonder if they managed to fit that particular plot in.

'Maybe when this is over,' said Matt, cutting into her reverie, 'we can spend some proper time together, getting to know each other better.'

'I'd like that,' said Philly, tears burning the back of her eyes. She realised with an aching heart that she not only meant what she said, but also regretted that it would never happen. Matt would either be arrested — or go away again, not having found what he wanted.

She was tempted to ask him outright what he had been looking for. If he wanted it that badly, she would give it to him. Then she remembered that everything in the house belonged to her and that if she needed money to keep the Hall maintained, she couldn't afford to go giving away priceless jewels or paintings. 'I ought to go and help Puck and Meg with dinner.'

'What can I do to help?'

'Perhaps you could just wait in the drawing room for the guests to come back down, and serve them drinks. If you don't mind, of course.'

'I don't mind at all. I'm glad to be useful. They won't be ready yet, so I'll check everything else is in place, shall I?'

'Yes, that would be really helpful. You have the script?'

Matt tapped his jacket pocket. 'I do indeed.'

Philly put her hand in her own pocket and fingered the attic key. It was not the right time to plant it just yet. Not with her and her friends busy in the kitchen. She smiled shyly at Matt and turned to go to the kitchen. But before she could walk away he caught her arm and pulled her back.

'I know you don't want to rush things, Philly, but since we've kissed already . . . '

Before she could argue, he had taken her in his arms. She was powerless to resist his charms. If, in that moment, he had asked for everything she owned, she would have agreed. She pulled away reluctantly. 'Well, I hardly think this is the correct behaviour between the headmaster and the games mistress,' she teased, trying to sound humorous, only to find that her voice trembled in her throat.

'It'll be our guilty secret,' murmured Matt. 'We could say that Dominique found out about us. It gives us both a motive.'

'You mustn't deviate from the script . . . Your motive, as the headmaster, is that you used to hang around with Kim Philby and all the other Cambridge traitors and you were still in the pay of the Russians. My motive, as the games mistress, is that I'd been stealing from school funds meant for buying hockey sticks in order to feed my alcoholism. Remember?'

'There's nothing wrong with ad-libbing. Especially if it gives me an excuse to kiss you. I could be the traitor, you could be the thief, yet we could still be secret lovers. Or perhaps you're blackmailing me into having a torrid fling.'

It sounded very seductive, the way he wrapped his tongue around the word torrid.

'You'll just confuse everyone,' said Philly, trying to sound more business-like. 'Stick to the script.'

'You're a very bossy games mistress.'

'Yes, and if you don't behave, I'll make you do a hundred push-ups.'

'Only a hundred? You're not so tough after all.'

'Get you, Bruce Willis!' Philly laughed, her dark mood instantly disappearing. No matter who or what Matt was, she couldn't help feeling good when she was with him. 'Now let me go and help out in the kitchen, or I'll have your motive as harassment of the innocent young games mistress.'

'I thought you said we couldn't change the script.'

'I said *you* couldn't change the script. I have writer's privileges.' Philly pulled away from his arms and headed towards the kitchen.

'Philly . . . ' Matt's voice sounded more serious.

'What is it?'

'You know I wouldn't, don't you?'

'Wouldn't what?'

'Harass you. I mean, if you gave me any sign you weren't interested in me, I wouldn't force my attentions on you.'

Things had suddenly become very serious again. Not least because no matter how hard Philly had tried, she clearly hadn't managed to appear reserved in Matt's company. Her longing for him must be all too apparent. 'I didn't mean to suggest that, Matt, I'm sorry. It was just a joke.'

'As long as you know that for sure.'

★ ★ ★

Rachel Jenson and her cameraman, Joe, arrived just before dinner. They set up the camera in the dining room. It was placed behind those who had stated they didn't wish to be featured on television, so that it only filmed the back of their heads. It meant that some of the original seating arrangements had to be changed at the last minute.

'It won't record sound,' Rachel explained to everyone. 'It will only record images, then I'll talk over it for the television report. So feel free to talk as you normally would. None of your deep, dark secrets will be revealed to the public.'

'Rachel,' said Matt, 'I saved you and Joe some characters to play. If you want to.'

'Ooh, yes please!' said Rachel.

Joe decided he would rather just be himself. Because he had to look after all the equipment he couldn't really devote his time to thinking up a back story and a motive.

'Remember that the bedrooms are

out of bounds, even to filming,' said Philly. 'It's only fair on the guests.'

'Of course, Philly.' Rachel smiled. 'We're not filming *Big Brother* here.'

'That's a relief,' said Frank Bennett, who was one of those who chose to sit with his back to the cameras. 'If I have to dress up and play silly games, I'm going home. It's bad enough having to cook when I'm on holiday.'

'I have to, every time we take the caravan to Morecombe,' pointed out Mrs Bennett.

'Now, shall we all get into character whilst we eat our soup?' suggested Matt.

Philly was grateful that he prevented yet another bickering session between the Bennetts. They were a direct contrast to the calm and obviously devoted Cunninghams.

'Why don't you start, Mrs Bennett?' Matt suggested.

'Ooh, I don't really know how to.'

'Start by telling us what role you're playing. Maybe the rest will come later.'

'Oh yes.' Mrs Bennett picked up her card. 'It says here that I'm the school nurse or doctor. Oh dear, I hate the sight of blood.' That caused a few raised eyebrows, especially as Mrs Bennett had already told nearly everyone that she was addicted to rather vicious American murder mysteries. 'Very well, I'm the school nurse. Just call me Matron. I came to work at the school in 1958 after doing a stint in Vietnam.'

'I don't think the Vietnam war had started then,' said her husband. 'And it was an American war.'

'I'm sure she means Korea,' said Matt, kindly.

'Yes!' Mrs Bennett beamed at him. 'It was Korea. I worked with the MASH four oh seven seven.'

'They were also Americans,' said Mr Bennett.

'There was a lot of crossover,' said Matt. 'The English and Americans have always come together in times of war.'

'Exactly,' said Mrs Bennett. She giggled. 'I had my heart broken after a torrid romance with Hawkeye Pierce.'

'Oh, I wish I'd been the school nurse now,' said Mrs Cunningham with a smile.

'Alan Alda was lovely, wasn't he?' Mrs Bennett beamed, having found a kindred spirit.

'He certainly was. And still is.'

'That's all I can think of for now,' added Mrs Bennett.

'You did great,' said Matt. Philly was struck by how easily he commanded the room. Everyone looked to him for guidance. 'Mr Bennett, do you want to tell us who you are?'

Frank Bennett sighed and picked up his card. 'It says here I'm the janitor. That's what I do in real life. I clean toilets at a local school. Couldn't I have had something more exciting?'

'But,' said Philly, cutting in before Matt could, 'the role can be as exciting as you want it to be. Maybe you're working undercover for the police or government.'

'Well I'm not going to tell you that at

the beginning of the story, am I?' said Frank. 'It'll give it away.'

'Quite right,' said Philly. 'But you could tell us some basic details about him . . . you.'

'Right, well he's . . . I'm a janitor and I have a wife who ran off with Alan blooming Alda.'

Everyone laughed, even though Frank Bennett had sounded genuinely peeved.

8

'Right, who wants to go next?' asked Philly. Matt really was taking over, and it unnerved her. She had to regain control, not just of the situation but of herself. Yet she had to concede that he knew how to deal with people. He had soothed Mrs Bennett's nerves, and whilst Frank Bennett was a tougher customer, he had still bowed to Matt's authority in the end.

Philly realised life would be much easier if Matt were not so charming and approachable. It put her off her guard, and she couldn't afford to do that with so much at stake.

'What about you, Mrs Cunningham? As you're playing yourself, perhaps you could tell us a little about the school when you worked here. Give us some background.'

'Yes, what a good idea,' said Mrs

Cunningham enthusiastically. Philly silently blessed her for her ability to get with the programme. She hoped that Mrs Cunningham's input would calm all the other nervous guests.

'It wasn't a big school,' said Mrs Cunningham. 'We only had about one hundred girls, aged from thirteen to eighteen. You can imagine the effect of all those hormones in one place. There were often tears, but there was a lot of laughter too.' Mrs Cunningham fell into a reverie, her eyes shining with remembrance. 'I loved working here . . . Not all the girls stayed till they were eighteen. Those whose parents could afford it sent their daughters to finishing schools in Switzerland. It was a pity really, as the headmistress of the time was quite progressive. She didn't think all girls should grow up to be the overdressed wives of diplomats, and nor did she think they should fall into the normal female professions of nurses and secretaries. One of our girls went on to become a heart surgeon in the late 1960s. Another was a famous actress . . . at least for a short time. She seemed to fall from grace very quickly.' Mrs Cunningham raised her eyebrows as if to suggest matters not fit for discussion in mixed company.

'What about the star of our show, Dominique?' asked Matt.

Mrs Cunningham shook her head. 'As I told Philly when we first met, it was very sad about Dominique. Not just that she went missing, but before that. I tried with that girl, I really did, but it seemed that no one could reach her. I understand that we're here for fun this weekend, and I don't wish to spoil that for anyone, but I did hope that coming back here would jog a memory of some sort. Something to solve the puzzle.'

'I hope you're not offended that we've arranged this,' said Philly, not for the first time.

'Oh no, dear. Life has to go on. It's only when you get to my age that you start living more in the past. I have to admit that I'm as intrigued by Dominique's disappearance as anyone else.'

'It was a man, I am sure,' said Monsieur De Lacey. 'It's always a man.'

'I thought the saying was *cherchez la femme*,' said Mrs Cunningham with a smile. 'Look for the woman. Except that Dominique was barely a woman. Little more than a child. Oh dear, I'm going to spoil things, I can tell. I promise to be more cheerful.' Mrs Cunningham surreptitiously wiped her eyes.

Philly's heart went out to her, and she felt a pang of guilt. The vicar's wife obviously did care about what happened to Dominique, yet they were using the details for entertainment.

'Come, Monsieur De Lacey, tell us why you're at the school,' Mrs Cunningham said with a smile. 'You must be a spy, with that accent.'

'I am hardly likely to admit it, Madame,' said the man with a wink. 'It says on the card that I am the teacher of mathematics. This is a pity as I don't add up well.' He shrugged in the way only a Frenchman could. It was very charming.

'Don't worry,' said Matt, 'we won't be testing you.'

'That is a relief! Before I came here to teach I worked . . . ah!' Monsieur De Lacey raised his hand. 'I shall not tell you yet. It's very sinister. If I had a moustache, I would most surely twirl it.'

'That's the spirit,' said Matt. Philly noticed he was taking over again, and yet she couldn't bring herself to object. She realised that she was having the time of her life. All her nerves about the weekend seemed to disappear as she enjoyed the way the guests gradually eased into their different roles.

'Reverend, would you like to tell us about your role, apart from the fact that we already know you are smitten with the pretty English teacher?' Matt continued.

'Whatever gave it away?' said the

Reverend, looking at his wife with loving eyes. 'Apparently I am a school governor, so I don't teach here at all. I merely come and stick my nose into things that don't concern me from time to time, and wonder why the girls are not fed bread and water.'

'Best thing for 'em,' said Mr Scattergood, who had been so quiet up until then Philly had almost forgotten he was there. She was glad to see that he at least took his flat cap off to come in to dinner. 'Kids today are spoiled rotten.'

'But we're not talking about kids today,' said Monsieur De Lacey. 'We're supposed to be in 1963. Is this not so?' he added with a shrug.

Philly couldn't help noticing a certain animosity between Mr Scattergood and the suave Frenchman. Two more different men she couldn't imagine. 'Yes, it is,' she agreed.

'I bet the girls at this school were spoilt,' said Scattergood. 'Little madams, the lot of them, living off daddy's riches.'

'Mrs Cunningham has already told us that some of the girls went on to be very successful,' said Philly.

'Yeah, some. But I bet the rest didn't. I bet they all married lords and rich men, and never got their hands dirty in their lives.'

Matt smiled, disarmingly. 'Are we to take from this that your role is that of a staunch socialist who would bring down the system, Mr Scattergood?'

'Too right it is. But it says on my card that I'm the cook.'

'We'll have to be careful you don't poison us all and overthrow the state then.'

'Don't give me any ideas, young man. You Americans are all the same.'

'Bravo, Mr Scattergood,' said Reverend Cunningham, clapping his hands together. 'A very convincing performance of an ardent communist.'

It was clearly a joke to try to lighten the mood, yet the more Philly thought about it, the more she wondered whether there was a real element of

147

play-acting to Mr Scattergood's performance. Except she would have sworn it had nothing to do with what it said on his card.

'Yes,' she said, clapping her own hands. 'You're a real find, Mr Scattergood. We'll have to employ you as a regular on our mystery weekends.'

'You'd be better off selling this house,' continued Scattergood. 'Let them turn it into a block of flats so that more families can live in it, and not just you and a couple of your equally privileged friends.'

Philly felt her cheeks flame. She knew that she was privileged to own such a wonderful house, but Mr Scattergood couldn't possibly know how difficult it was to pay for the upkeep, or that Meg and Puck were far from being privileged. She wanted to rise to the defence of her friends, but felt it would be inappropriate in front of all the other guests. Just because Scattergood behaved badly, it didn't mean she had to.

'Maybe you got a bit too much into character there, Mr Scattergood,' said Matt. His voice sounded strained, and somewhat dangerous. His fingers tightened around his wine glass, turning his knuckles white. 'And maybe you owe the young lady an apology, since you're a guest in her house.'

Scattergood glared at Matt, but was resolutely out-glared. 'Of course — I'm sorry, Miss Sanderson. I get a bit carried away sometimes. I meant no offence.'

'None taken,' said Philly, smiling tightly. Matt's defence of her had been even more shocking than Scattergood's verbal attack. It churned up her emotions in ways she found disturbing. 'Shall we all take coffee in the drawing room now? Then we can hear some more stories and watch the first part of our mystery.'

'Wow,' Rachel Jenson whispered to Philly as they were leaving the dining room, 'this is turning into an interesting weekend. I wish we'd been recording old Stalin over there. As you said, he's a real find. I didn't know people like him still existed.' Rachel nudged Philly and winked. 'I could say the same about your handsome American headmaster. With those looks, they're going to love him back at the television station. I reckon if you can persuade Matt to do more of these weekends, you'll have women breaking down the doors to get in. That's if the channel don't snap him up. I reckon he could just stand in front of the camera all day, giving that smile and talking about the weather, and the female populace would still be enthralled.'

'We only have the very best at Bedlington Hall,' Philly quipped, deeply concerned that the lovely Rachel Jenson really did seem to fancy Matt. It would solve all Philly's problems if he reciprocated — but that didn't mean she wanted it to happen.

★ ★ ★

'Our story begins in early 1963,' said Matt, standing with his back to the fireplace. As the fire crackled in the hearth, casting a warm glow over the dimly lit room, the guests sipped their coffee and listened avidly. Puck had come from the kitchen to join them, his role that of one of the schoolchildren, looking comical in a blazer and short trousers, with a black school cap sitting on the back of his head. 'It is a time of Cold War and the Space Race,' Matt continued, 'with America and Russia vying for supremacy in both. It would be another six years before man stood on the moon, but the excitement of the challenge enthused everyone. Science fiction had prospered throughout the fifties, particularly in films like *The Day The Earth Stood Still*, and it led to questions about life on other planets.'

'Ooh, I like that one,' said Mrs Bennett. 'Michael Rennie. They don't make them like him any more.' Her husband shushed her, but Matt gave her his most charming grin.

'I love that film too,' he said. 'Much better than the recent remake.' Philly wondered at his ability to disarm people with a few well-chosen words, and a dazzling smile. He had also quickly weighed up his largely middle-aged audience, knowing just what references would appeal to them. 'Britain has finally recovered from World War Two, heading into an age of prosperity. A group of young men who had been honing their craft in a club in Germany had just burst onto the music scene. I am, of course, talking about The Beatles.'

'I had a huge crush on Paul,' sighed Mrs Cunningham. 'Still have, really!'

'Oh, it was Ringo for me,' said Mrs Bennett. 'He wasn't as pretty as the others, but he reminded me of my husband.'

Mr Bennett harrumphed in the corner and muttered something about playing the drums better than Ringo Starr. 'Let the man get on with his talk,' he said, grumpily.

'I don't mind,' said Matt. 'It all adds colour to the proceedings, and helps us to get to know each other. Where was I? Oh yeah, The Beatles. So that was the larger picture. We now bring you to the smaller picture. A boarding school in Shropshire. Not one of the top seeded schools, but still a good school, teaching the children of the nouveau riche. Before Bedlington Hall was a school, it had been a military hospital during the war, for officers recuperating from dreadful injuries. In between times it had been owned by a Colonel Trefusis, who had died mysteriously.'

This was something that Philly had learned only recently from Mrs Cunningham.

'My husband and I found his killer, you know,' the vicar's wife said. 'But it was a long time afterwards. It was how we first met, actually.'

'Many years before that, during Victorian times, it had been owned by Lord and Lady Bedlington,' Matt continued, 'before passing into the hands of the Sanderson family at the turn of the century. They couldn't afford to live in the Hall, so went to live cheaply abroad whilst they leased the hall to the hospital and then the school.' He went quiet for a moment to give people time to digest what he had said. He caught Philly's eye and mouthed, 'How am I doing?'

She put her thumb up in appreciation. He was doing very well. 'And it's into this picture we introduce seventeen-year-old Dominique DuPont.' At his words, the door flew open, causing everyone to jump. A plain-looking girl walked in. Meg had done her hair up in pigtails, covered her face with freckles, and plumped out her tummy with cushions, looking nothing like Philly's normally pretty friend. She stood silently, illuminated by the light from the hall, whilst Matt finished his monologue.

'Dominique, as you can see, is a plain girl, lacking in social graces. She doesn't make friends easily, and guards her food parcels as if her life depends

154

on eating the entire contents. One teacher, Mrs Cunningham, feels sorry for her and tries to reach out to the girl, but everyone else considers poor Dominique to be tiresome.' Matt's voice lowered in tone, adding more drama to his words. 'One morning, Dominique disappeared. Completely. And not just Dominique, but all her belongings. It was as if she never existed. For years afterwards, girls at the school would say they had seen her. Some believed they heard her moving about upstairs long after she had gone.' Matt became more business-like for a moment. 'Just to be clear, the events of this weekend are entirely fictional. We don't know what happened to the girl. Your task this weekend, ladies and gentleman, is to come up with a solution for Dominique's disappearance drawn entirely from your imaginations. And now,' Matt gestured with his hand, 'let our story begin.'

The lights in the room became brighter. The guests looked at each other, wondering who could have done it, not realising that Puck had a remote control unit in his blazer pocket.

'Oh, this is good,' said Mrs Bennett.

'We'll see,' said Mr Bennett.

Dominique walked forward and stood in front of Matt. 'Monsieur Cassell, I weesh to speak wiz you.'

'Not now, Dominique. As you can see I have guests.' Matt rubbed his cheek awkwardly, as if caught off guard.

'No, it eez important zat I speak wiz you now.'

Monsieur De Lacey chuckled and sipped his coffee. Philly winced, guessing he was laughing at Meg's dreadful French accent. She was sure her friend had been practising. The effect was less Catherine Deneuve, and more *'Allo 'Allo*.

'Eet will be bad for you, if you do not speak wiz me,' said Dominique firmly.

'Are you threatening me, Dominique?' asked Matt.

Dominique turned around and addressed the room. 'I am threatening all of you. I have ze secrets.'

'Are zey 'idden in ze portrait of ze Madonna wiz ze big . . . ' Frank Bennett couldn't get any further because his wife nudged him fiercely in the ribs.

'Behave!' she said. He slumped in his seat, looking glum.

'Ah,' said Dominique, truly in character, 'you may mock me, Monsieur Janitor, but I have ze secrets about you too. I know where you go on ze Saturday night.'

Mr Bennett looked a bit taken aback, his eyes darting upwards to where Dominique stood in front of him. The room was filled with uncomfortable coughs and embarrassed chuckles, until the other guests realised it was indeed a joke and part of the entertainment. It took Mr Bennett a few seconds longer to get the joke. 'You watch yourself, Madam-moiselle,' he said, in a jocular fashion. His voice became lower and deeper, sounding like the man who did the movie trailers, but he couldn't stop his lips from twisting into a grin as he spoke. 'I don't make threats, I make promises.'

Philly's eyes widened in surprise. She had expected Mr Bennett to be difficult and grumpy. She smiled with relief when she saw him nudge his wife and say, 'It's a bit of a laugh, all this pretending, innit?'

Dominique pointed around the room. 'I know ze truth about all of you, and I will tell if you do not leesten to me. Something bad eez going to 'appen . . . '

She flounced out of the room, and was rewarded with a loud round of applause.

'And that,' said Matt, 'was the last time anyone saw Dominique in public. Some girls saw her go into her bedroom at night, but she didn't turn up for breakfast the next morning. What happened to her? That is up to you. The clues are out there, so you're welcome to start hunting for them as soon as you are ready.'

Philly looked around the room at

rapt faces. Things were going much better than she'd ever dreamed. Even Meg's dodgy sitcom accent hadn't dampened their guests' enthusiasm. After a moment's silence, everyone started chatting avidly.

Philly's gaze alighted on Mrs Cunningham. The old lady looked sad and confused, shaking her head as she spoke intently to her husband. Philly rushed over to her, concerned.

'I hope it hasn't upset you, Mrs Cunningham.'

'No, dear, that's not it. It's just that . . . oh, do you know how it is when you only realise something long after the event.'

'You mean about Dominique's disappearance?'

'No, that's not it. I think it's Monsieur De Lacey being here that has brought it to mind. That and your fellow actress's awful French accent. Oh, please, don't think I'm being rude.'

'No, not at all. It was a little bit rubbish. She hasn't had time to practise,' Philly added, defending her best friend.

'I'm not complaining. Only noticing.'

'What is it, darling?' asked Reverend Cunningham.

Mrs Cunningham shook her head. 'I need to think about it a bit more. To collect my thoughts. I could easily be misremembering . . . '

'Oh for goodness sake, darling,' said the Reverend. 'You know darn well that when people say things like that in films they end up dead. So out with it.'

Mrs Cunningham smiled. 'I hardly think anyone is going to kill me for it now. After fifty years there's no one left to care about poor Dominique . . . except me.'

'And me,' said Philly, with the pang of guilt that was becoming all too familiar. She began to wonder whether using Dominique's disappearance as the basis for their story was a good idea. After all, it was a human being they were dealing with. But mostly, Philly had become fond of Mrs

Cunningham and didn't want her to be distressed.

It was a dangerous game, playing around with the past. It was possible that the wrong people would be hurt by it.

Almost as if she had wished for it, she felt a comforting arm on her shoulder, and turned her head to see Matt smiling down. 'I think that went great,' he said.

9

'I wish I could stop liking him,' Philly said to Meg, later that night. They sat on the edge of Philly's bed, chatting. 'And I should be getting you this,' she added, pointing to the cocoa. 'You're the one who did all the hard work.'

'It wasn't so hard,' said Meg, 'talking in a lousy French accent and behaving like a typical over-emotional teenager. It certainly takes me back. Matt worked hard tonight, didn't he?'

'Yes he did.' Philly struggled to erase the memory of his bemused face when she had dashed up the stairs before he could kiss her goodnight.

'We know what you mean about him though, love,' said Meg. 'Me and Puck were just saying that we like him despite everything. I suppose that's the mark of a true conman. People like them even whilst they're being conned.'

'You don't think I could have mistaken the phone call, do you? Maybe he meant something different.'

'I thought you distinctly heard him say he wanted to get into the attic and it would get the person on the other end of the phone what they wanted.'

Philly sighed. 'Yes, that's what I heard, and it's no good fooling myself otherwise. We'll have to try to find time to plant the attic key.' She reached into the pocket of her blue satin 1950s-style dress, and then in the other pocket, becoming frantic. 'It's gone.'

She jumped up off the bed and looked around the floor, then threw some of the covers off the bed, also lifting the pillows. 'It's gone, Meg! I had it, I'm sure I did.'

'You didn't take it out when you changed out of your jeans then forgot to put it in your dress pocket?' said Meg. She also stood up and began scouting the floor and the bed for the missing key.

'No, I didn't. I knew these pockets

were too shallow for that key, but I liked the dress.' Actually, she had worn it in the hopes that Matt would like it, too. And he had, whispering that she looked beautiful when she first arrived in the dining room.

'Come on, we'll retrace your steps. It's bound to be around here somewhere.'

'He put his arm around me,' said Philly, sadly. 'When I was seeing to Mrs Cunningham. He put his arm around me. Perhaps he saw it sticking out from my pocket and took it.'

'It might not be that,' said Meg. 'It's not as if it was on prominent display, as we intended to leave it. I'm sure you've just dropped it. Come on, let's go and look for it, otherwise you won't sleep for worrying.'

The two friends went downstairs. Most of the guests had gone to bed but a couple were in the drawing room, having late night drinks. They could hear them discussing the case and the clues found so far, and stood by the door trying to work out the best time to go in and disturb them.

'So we have her trunk, thrown in the shrubbery,' said old Mr Graham gravely.

'That's not exactly disappearing without a trace, is it?' said Mr Bennett. Mrs Bennett had retired some time ago.

'I suppose not,' said Mr Graham, 'but it's interesting that they have the actual trunk here, isn't it? A real piece of criminal history there. I wonder that the young lady doesn't sell it to the Black Museum.'

'What is this Black Museum?' That was Monsieur De Lacey's distinctive voice.

'Oh, it's where the police keep all the gruesome finds from murders,' said Frank Bennett, salaciously. 'Got some right good stuff down there, they have. I took our Irene down for our last wedding anniversary.'

'Very romantic,' said Monsieur De Lacey, dryly.

'Our Irene loves that sort of thing,'

said Frank, defensively. 'You should see all the books she's got on murders. Other women read Mills and Boon. My wife reads about Jack the Ripper. That's how I knew she'd prefer this to Majorca.'

'How did you come to learn of this place?' asked De Lacey. 'I believe it's not your first visit.'

'Nah, we came to the last weekend. It wasn't as good as this time, I'll tell you. They seem to have got their act together. Anyway, our Irene used to go to school here, so we know the area well.'

'Here?'

'Well, no, not here at Bedlington Hall. In the village school.'

Philly and Meg exchanged surprised glances. That was something they didn't know.

'Did she know Dominique?' De Lacey asked Frank.

'No, she was a bit younger. Our Irene, that is. Only about five years old at the time. But she knew about the case and reckons she remembers seeing the girl. I don't know how much a five-year-old would remember. Mind you, she didn't want me to tell folks that.'

'Why not?'

'Oh, well the thing is, our Irene's brother, Harry, used to hang around Bedlington Hall a lot. Got into trouble for it and ended up in prison.'

'He was seeing a girl?'

'Oh, no,' said Frank. 'Nothing like that. He used to come up and nick stuff. Vegetables from the garden, sports equipment, what have you. He was only a petty thief. Not much older than fourteen, but he knew his way around a door lock. Anyway, one night they caught him on the premises with some money that didn't belong to him. He swore it had been given to him by some bloke, loitering at the school that night, who wanted Harry to keep quiet. But no one believed him. He couldn't name the bloke and couldn't really say what the fella looked like, it being dark and all that. All he knew was that the other chap was meeting a really pretty girl. One of the girls from the school maybe, though Harry says that from what he saw of her, she was too sophisticated to be a schoolgirl. More like one of the young teachers. Maybe that Mrs Cunningham when she worked here. I reckon she was a bit of a looker in her day. Still got a naughty sparkle in her eyes. Anyway, our Irene doesn't like to talk about it. She always says Harry was set up, like.'

'What happened to the brother of your wife?' asked Monsieur De Lacey.

'He kept getting into trouble all through the sixties. Then do you know what? He emigrated to Australia, turned over a new leaf and he's as rich as King blooming Midas now. Not that he even bothers to send us a Christmas card. Our Irene was farmed out to relatives when her mam and dad died, yet Harry's never lifted a finger to help her. Ah well, I'd better be getting to bed. It's a long day of sleuthing tomorrow and I think I have to cook blooming dinner an' all. Who ever heard of coming to stay in a hotel and having to cook your own dinner?'

Philly and Meg jumped back into the shadows, whilst the three men came out of the drawing room and went up the stairs to bed.

'Do you think . . . ' Meg started to say, before Philly silenced her with a look.

'We don't know who else is around,' she whispered. 'Wait till we're back upstairs.'

As Philly feared, Mr Graham, Frank Bennett and Monsieur De Lacey were not the only ones in the drawing room. A minute or so later, Mr Scattergood left the room. He stood at the bottom of the stairs, looking up thoughtfully. Philly was terrified he would turn around and see them, but all his attention was elsewhere. With a deep sigh, he climbed the stairs.

When he had gone out of sight, they searched the drawing room, the kitchen, the main hall and the dining room, to no avail. 'Someone must have it,' said Philly. 'And if we don't get upstairs soon, we might miss them.'

The two girls crept up the dimly lit staircase, even though there was no real reason they shouldn't be walking around their own home. Meg went to tell Puck that she would be sitting with Philly for a while, then the two girls sat in Philly's darkened bedroom, waiting to see if anything happened.

Philly got an extra duvet out of her wardrobe, so Meg could wrap herself up and they huddled at either end of Philly's bed, chatting quietly.

'Mrs Bennett's brother,' Meg remarked. 'There's something funny there, don't you think?'

'Yes, I thought exactly the same. What was he up to? If he didn't meet a man, that means he was up to no good here. If he did meet a stranger, why did the stranger pay him off? I wonder if Dominique saw young Harry and he silenced her later.'

'I wish we could find out when it happened,' said Meg.

'We'll try to get it out of Mrs Bennett. Assuming she remembers the date. She was very young at the time.'

'But even if she only knows it was around the time Dominique went missing, it might be relevant.' Meg smiled widely. 'Oh, Philly, I can't believe that we're actually talking about a real live mystery here. Oh, I know we chose the Dominique story, but the fact that we may have another link to her besides Mrs Cunningham . . .'

'I know,' Philly replied. 'It's turning out to be exciting. I just hope . . . well, I hope that Matt isn't involved.'

'He could hardly be involved in the disappearance of a girl nearly fifty years ago, Philly. It had to have been twenty years before he was born.'

'But maybe his parents were. Or some people he knows. You know these mafia types. They bear a grudge for a long time.'

'Oh, so we've decided he's the mafia

now, have we? He's a bit tall for Al Pacino, and a bit too un-Italian looking for that matter, too!'

'Russian mafia?'

'As wonderful as Matt's cheekbones undoubtedly are, I don't think they're Slavic.'

'Polish?' Philly offered.

'Yeah, maybe. Or perhaps even Welsh.'

'Is there a Welsh mafia?'

'Of course. You should see my aunties if anyone upsets them. You wouldn't want to cross them, I can tell you. Mind you, they only ply people with cups of tea, fruit cake and a good talking to, basically mothering them to death. It's not up there with a horse's head, but it is much nicer to wake up to.'

Philly laughed. 'I'm glad you're here, talking to me. It stops me worrying about stuff.'

'Things will work out, one way or another, I'm sure of it.'

★ ★ ★

It was in the early hours, and they had both started to doze, when Philly heard footsteps overhead. Philly's eyes snapped open. 'Meg,' she hissed. She nudged her friend with her foot. 'Meg, did you hear that?'

'Wha . . . huh?' Meg's eyes half opened. 'Puck . . . '

Philly giggled and kicked her friend again. 'It's me you idiot!'

'Oh.' Meg sat up, more awake. 'Sorry, forgot where I was for a moment.'

'I heard someone upstairs and if we don't get moving, we'll miss them.'

The girls tiptoed to the bedroom door, which made a prodigious amount of noise when Philly opened it, as did their footsteps. Every floorboard made its own unique sound as they walked along the hallway towards the staircase leading to the upper rooms.

'I reckon,' Meg whispered, 'if we stop trying to be quiet, we won't make nearly as much noise.'

'Shh.' Philly put her finger to her lips, trying not to laugh. She had a desperate need to giggle, because the situation seemed so ridiculous. Yet it was not funny. Any minute now, she might come face to face with Matt, and by the same token, face to face with her fears about his motives.

She had no idea how she would deal with it. The most obvious thing to do would be to throw him out of the house, yet her typical British good manners almost forbade it.

She hated the idea of a confrontation and was sorely tempted to turn around and go straight back to bed, pulling the duvet over her head and pretending none of it had ever happened. If she did that, how could she face him the next day? Assuming he hung around once he found what he was looking for.

She paused at the bottom of the staircase. 'What is it?' whispered Meg.

'I'm not sure I want to know,' Philly murmured back. 'I mean, what if it is him?'

'Who else could it be? Puck wouldn't go up there at night. He has access to it all day if he's bothered. None of the other guests could possibly know what's in the attic. If there *is* anything up there.'

'No, I suppose not.'

'Look,' whispered Meg, 'if it is him, I'll throw him out. You don't have to. It's better that way. I don't care if I offend him.'

'Neither do I!' Philly hissed.

'Darling, you're the sort of person who says 'sorry' when someone else treads on your toe. I can easily imagine you saying, 'I'm so sorry I caught you trying to steal from my house. Let's have a cup of tea and talk about it.'' Meg affected a very good impersonation of Philly's soft vocal tones.

'I'm not that much of a pushover.'

'Yeah, actually, you are. Especially where he's concerned.'

'You're right. I know you are. I just wish it didn't have to hurt so much.'

'I know, sweetie, but the sooner it's over the better. I'll give him what for, don't you worry. Come on, otherwise he'll hear us and be gone before we get there.'

'He'd have to come past us,' said Philly. 'There's no other way down, apart from through the dormer window in the attic, and it's a long drop to the ground.'

They took the stairs slowly, but as with the floorboards, each step creaked insanely, almost as if they were waking a sleeping animal. They reached the top and looked along the hallway to the attic. The door was open, and they could hear someone moving about inside.

'Right,' said Meg. 'We've got him. Come on . . . '

The girls instinctively held hands as they neared the door. There was only one old-fashioned electric bulb in the attic and it didn't emit much light, especially in a room packed to the rafters with old furniture and trunks. They could hear the sound of rustling inside, as if someone were shifting around little items like books and clothing.

'Who is it?' said Philly, when they reached the open doorway. She reached for the door and took the key out, somehow feeling safer with it in her hands. She slipped it into her dressing gown pocket. 'Who is in there?'

The rustling stopped immediately and all became silent. It felt like something of a stand off, as the girls were too terrified to move forward, and whoever was in the attic didn't want to come out. 'Come out of there now,' said Meg. 'We shan't call the police or anything. We just want you to leave quietly.'

'Yeah, that told him,' Philly whispered, grinning at Meg's idea of giving Matt what for.

'Shut up.' Meg playfully punched Philly on the arm. 'If you don't come out, we're coming in to get you. We've already telephoned the police . . . '

'You just said we wouldn't,' Philly murmured. 'Make your mind up.' She imagined that Matt would be laughing his head off around now. He was a big strong man, who could easily knock down two young women, and they hadn't shown themselves to be very brave so far, standing at the door, offering to let him just walk out of there. She began to wish they had woken Puck, not just for moral support, but also for some extra muscle.

Then she rallied herself. They were modern young women. They didn't need a man to take care of them. 'Right,' she said, sounding braver than she felt, 'we're coming in.'

She took a step forward, just as something warm and furry brushed past her bare feet, causing her to scream at the top of her voice.

'What!' said Meg.

'Something just brushed my legs. Ugh, it was horrible.'

The landing light came on and there were heavy footsteps on the stairs. Within seconds a man came into view on the landing. He was dressed in pyjama trousers and very little else. 'What is it?' he said. 'What's wrong?

Are you all right, Philly, darling?'

'Matt? How? I mean . . . ' She could barely put into words how pleased she was to see him standing at the top of the stairs and not in the attic. But if he wasn't in the attic, who was?

Philly and Meg looked at each other, both wondering what was happening.

10

'We've done a thorough search through the attic and there was no one there,' said Matt. 'I'm sure it was just a rat you heard moving around up there, darling.'

Philly and Meg had waited in the kitchen whilst Matt and Puck went to the attic. Some of the guests had come from their room on hearing Philly scream, but soon went back in bed. The girls sat at the table with hot drinks, having only just calmed their shattered nerves.

'Just a rat?' said Philly, shuddering. 'I'm not sure that's very comforting. It was huge.' She didn't ask Matt how a rat could possibly manage to grab a set of keys and unlock the door. She knew from his phone call that he had been interested in the attic, and still didn't know whether to trust him.

Whilst Philly and Meg had been

alone in the kitchen, Philly had said, 'Maybe Matt just went downstairs for a minute and didn't realise we were up there.'

'But someone else was in there too,' said Meg. 'We heard them, didn't we?'

'Do you think he might have an accomplice?' Philly seriously wondered if things could get worse.

'Maybe. If not, then it means that someone else in the house is interested in the attic.'

That was definitely under the heading of things getting worse. Who could they trust if anyone staying at the house could have picked the keys up? She tried to remember who had come out of their rooms, but she had been so shaken, when walking downstairs, she could not remember. Besides, not all the rooms were in a direct line with the staircase and upper hall. Some were around corners, and in the other wings.

'Did you check the dormer window?' she asked Matt, as she sipped a soothing cup of tea.

'Yep, and it was tightly shut, but I don't think anyone would climb out onto the roof. They'd be crazy to in this terrible weather, with all that snow lying up there. Even if they didn't slip and break a few bones, they could freeze to death up there.'

'I suppose so. Has Puck locked the attic back up?'

'Yes, don't worry. And maybe it's a good idea to keep it locked in future.'

'Hmm, yes.' Philly nodded. It had been locked, but she didn't want to tell Matt that. Let him think they had accidentally left it open. Otherwise she would have to explain about losing the key, and that might lead to why she had the key in her pocket attached to a big label saying 'attic' in the first place.

'I'm sure it's nothing, darling,' said Matt, putting his hand over hers. Why did that have to feel so good? It would be much easier if he were ugly and unapproachable, rather than a solid block of gorgeous, seemingly warm-hearted manhood that she would rather like to cuddle up to and be comforted by.

'But maybe you ought to contact someone tomorrow about putting some rat traps up there,' he went on.

'Yes, good idea. I had no idea we had rats, did you, Meg? I'm sure there are some environmental health rules about them, regarding running what is essentially a hotel. You don't think they'll close us down, do you?' It was just one more thing for Philly to worry about.

'I'm sure they won't.' Matt squeezed her hand again. 'I think you'll be allowed some leeway in getting rid of them first.' He looked at her squarely before saying, 'It's a good job you and Meg were having a late night chat. I'd hate to think of you going up there all alone.'

'Yes, isn't it just?' said Meg, before Philly could speak. It was just as well Meg spoke. With the feel of Matt's hand on hers, Philly was rendered speechless. 'We often do, don't we, sweetie? It's nice to have a girlie chat at the end of the day. Then we went and dozed off, talking about . . . oh, who was it?'

'Gerard Butler,' said Philly.

'That's him. Gerard Butler.'

'Does he live around here?' asked Matt.

The girls laughed. 'No, silly, he's an actor,' said Philly.

'Someone you know?'

'We wish!' said Meg. 'No, he's out of our league.'

'Well, that's a relief. I don't want to have to challenge him to a duel to win Philly's affections,' Matt quipped in reply.

'They're not on about Gerard Butler again?' said Puck, coming into the kitchen. He handed the attic key to Philly. She winked at him, silently blessing him for backing up the Gerard Butler discussion.

'Yes, he seems to be a favourite topic of conversation,' said Matt, smiling.

'You have no idea. Especially since he played the *Phantom*.'

'The phantom what?'

'*Of the Opera.*'

'Oh . . . ' Matt laughed. 'I must have missed that one.'

'Yeah,' said Puck. 'You only think women want a tall, dark handsome man. What they really want is a short, stocky baritone with half his face covered. If only I'd known it was so easy I wouldn't have had all the plastic surgery.' He sucked his cheeks in, and crossed his eyes.

'Of course,' said Meg, mischievously, 'if half your face were covered, Puck, it would be a blessing to us all. Especially since the surgery didn't go so well.'

'Oh, there she goes again with the insults.' Puck folded over as if he had been shot by an arrow. 'You wait, Matt. A woman might be all sweetness and light to you in the beginning, but get to know her better and she'll be insulting you on a daily basis. Yet you dare mention that they have a big bum and see what happens . . . Not that I'm saying that at all, darling,' he added hastily, picking up Meg's hand and kissing it.

Philly was surprised to hear Puck talk as if Matt would be around forever. Despite laughing, and putting on a brave face, it saddened her. Because she wouldn't be getting to know Matt at all. Not once he had found what he was looking for in the attic.

'Oh,' she said, wanting to take the conversation onto other matters, 'I overheard something interesting tonight.' Without telling either Puck or Matt the full details of how she and Meg came to be eavesdropping outside the drawing room, she explained what Frank Bennett had said about his wife's brother. 'I wondered,' she said, when she had finished, 'whether it might be possible to get him on the phone and see what he remembers from that time.'

'Good idea,' nodded Matt. 'But what about Mrs Cunningham? If she was a teacher here at that time, she might remember the details.'

'Of course!' Philly rolled her eyes. 'I hadn't thought of that. I'll have to do it when Irene Bennett isn't around. Are they on the same kitchen duty, Puck?'

'They were,' he replied, 'but it can easily be changed. Leave it to me.'

'You're determined to solve the mystery of Dominique, aren't you?' Matt said to Philly. 'The real mystery, that is.'

'I'd just like to know why a young girl just up and disappeared from my house.'

'But an old man was murdered here too, according to Mrs Cunningham anyway.'

'That was solved ages ago. The murderer went to prison. It's not related, by the way. Mrs Cunningham said so. We just threw that into the script as a red herring, along with the mention of Cold Wars and Space Races.'

'Yeah,' said Puck. 'We're actually leaving the solution to the guests. We're going to give a prize for the most imaginative.'

'It could have been the old man's

ghost rattling about in the attic,' said Meg.

'Thanks so much,' said Philly, almost choking on her drink. 'Ghosts were the one thing I hadn't thought about! Now I shan't sleep at all.'

'It would solve a lot of problems, though,' said Meg, pointedly. Only Philly and Puck knew that she was talking about Matt now.

'I guess you could charge for ghost tours then,' Matt said, frowning slightly.

Suddenly there was a heavy thud outside the back door. The girls squealed, whilst the men emitted a manlier 'Whoa.'

'What the . . . ' Puck went to unlock the door, letting a blast of icy air into the kitchen. Matt stood up, ready for action but still holding Philly's hand in his.

'What is it?' asked Philly. She only noticed she'd gripped Matt's hand tighter when he smiled down at her.

'A little blood to the fingers would be nice,' he said.

'Sorry.' Philly tried to let go completely, but he wouldn't loosen his own grip.

He winked at her. 'I'm not.'

'Some snow has fallen off the roof,' said Puck. 'I reckon we're in for a thaw.'

'What a pity,' said Meg. 'I was starting to look forward to a white Christmas.'

The friends all said goodnight, and Matt insisted on walking Philly to her room. When he embraced her, she welcomed his kiss, wanting to enjoy, if only for a short time, the comfort and safety of his arms.

'You hear any ghosts, darling, you just holler for me,' he whispered in her ear, before going back to his own room.

In the early hours, Philly awoke slightly when she thought she heard the muffled tinkle of breaking glass, followed by one of the guests swearing. She decided that someone had probably dropped a glass in their room whilst getting a drink. Exhausted by the excitement so far, she fell back into a deep slumber.

★ ★ ★

'I don't care if you have a note from your mother, Puck Jenson,' Philly said in her best jolly-hockey-sticks voice, 'you're still doing PT. Of course, if you didn't spend so much time behind the bike sheds, drinking Guinness and kissing all the girls, you might feel fitter in the mornings.'

'Aw, Miss,' said Puck, doing a good impression of a stroppy teenage boy. 'PT is boring.'

They had turned the ballroom into a makeshift gym. There was no equipment, apart from a couple of hula hoops and some tennis balls that they found in the garden shed. Bill Haley and the Comets were playing on the music system, and Philly was talking the guests through a few very light dance-based exercises. Not everyone had joined this part of the weekend, due to health problems or most likely apathy, but even they wouldn't have found the programme too strenuous.

'And run around in a circle,' said Philly, thoroughly enjoying herself as she followed the last of the stragglers. She needed the exercise too, not having had much sleep, and found it invigorating. 'Now do-si-do.'

'What does that mean, Miss?' asked Puck.

'I haven't got a clue, Jenson, just get on with it.'

The guests laughed.

'You should be jiving to this,' said Mr Graham. His friends, the Bennetts got out of the morning exercise by dint of being the janitor and the nurse. Mr Graham had drawn the short straw of being a pupil. 'I bet none of you young 'uns can jive.'

'I can,' said Philly. 'So come on, Mr Graham, put your money where your mouth is and show the others how it's done.'

Philly took his hand, and they began

jiving, whilst everyone clapped and cheered.

'Mind you,' said Mr Graham, breathlessly, as they jigged around, 'in my younger days I could have picked you up and thrown you over my shoulder.'

'Please don't do that now,' said Philly, alarmed. 'I'm not sure I could survive it, let alone you.' She spun around, laughing. 'Come on, everyone, join in. Just follow me and Mr Graham. That means you, Mr Cassell, lurking by the door there. Some of these young ladies are short of partners.'

'I'm the headmaster, I don't have to do Phys Ed. Perk of the job,' he smirked.

'I'll have you know it's called PT in these parts. Or at least it was in the sixties. Don't bring your Americanisms here. Pretty soon we'll be overrun with burger and coffee bars. Oh yeah — I forgot. We already are.'

'Okay, ladies, which one of you wants me?' asked Matt.

'All of us!' said one woman, whose

name Philly couldn't quite remember.

'I guess you'd all better take a number, then.'

At that moment the track changed to a slower song, *To Know Him Is To Love Him*.

'Saved by the bell,' said Matt, taking the woman into his arms, and dancing her gently around the room. Philly tried to ignore the pang of jealousy. After all, the woman was in her late forties, albeit very attractive. The other guests partnered up, mostly with the ladies having to partner each other, due to a lack of men. Those who managed to dance with Matt and Puck, who were the youngest and best-looking men in the room, looked very smug indeed.

'If you don't mind, Miss Sanderson, I'll sit down now,' said Mr Graham.

'Oh, of course,' said Philly, feeling guilty because all her attention had been on Matt and not her dance partner. 'I haven't overdone it, have I? I don't want you to be unwell.'

'No, lass, you're doing all right. It's a

long time since I danced with a pretty young woman. It's made my day, it has. I'm just not as young as I used to be. I reckon one and a half songs is my limit nowadays.'

'Between you and me,' Philly whispered, 'I'm worn out too. So we'll both have a rest.'

Mr Graham went to sit down, and Philly was about to go and do the same when Matt caught her arm.

'Not so quick, Miss Sanderson.' He had somehow lost his partner, and pulled Philly into his arms, sweeping her around the floor. 'You can spare one dance with the headmaster, whilst we plot and scheme our torrid affair.'

'I thought I told you to stick to the script.'

'You also told me I could improvise. I'm ad-libbing disgracefully,' he whispered.

'You are a disgrace. I wonder how you ever got to be a headmaster,' she teased in return.

'I lied my way into the job.'

Philly became serious for a moment. 'Did you?'

Matt laughed. 'Hey, remember we're supposed to be having fun here. This is a cosy mystery weekend, not . . . what's that television programme with all the miserable people you Brits love so much?'

'*EastEnders?*'

'That's the one. *EastEnders.*'

'I played a stallholder in that once. 'A paaand of apples and pears,'' Philly intoned in her best East London accent. 'Get yer jellied eels and custard right 'ere.'

'Jellied eels and custard? I think I'll pass on that one.'

'It was something like that. I forget. They did consider me as a love interest for one of the Mitchell boys, but considering their wives and girlfriends have a life expectancy of about thirty, I turned them down.'

'I don't think they actually kill them though, do they? The actress just goes on to better things.'

'You don't know the BBC's attention to detail,' Philly quipped. 'Anyway, to some people death is appearing on *I'm A Celebrity*. I haven't sunk quite that low yet. Well . . . ' she looked around her and wondered just where on the list an actress at a murder mystery weekend came. Probably somewhere below Z.

'You're doing okay,' said Matt, pulling her closer. The song had changed again, to Buddy Holly singing *That'll Be The Day*, which was a little more up tempo, but they still danced close together. 'You're a fantastic hostess, you know. Everyone likes you, and you genuinely care about making people happy. I saw you with Mr Graham. He's smitten, as we all are.'

'I don't think Mr Scattergood likes me,' said Philly, trying to ignore the hammering in her heart. 'He thinks I should be flogged for owning this house.'

'He'd have to get past me first. Besides, I think he's the kind of guy who says things for effect. I wouldn't

196

take too much notice of him.'

'I just want things to go well,' Philly said. 'Not to be rich, but to make enough to keep the house and to live on, so I'm not dependent on anyone.'

'That's a good goal to have, but . . . '

'What?'

'Well, it doesn't hurt to turn to others for help, sometimes.'

'I know that. This is why I've got Meg and Puck to help me.'

'You don't just have them, Philly.'

She struggled to ignore the inference in his word, telling herself that they meant nothing. 'They have their own lives, you know? I can't expect them to stay forever. Puck could be one of the best actors in Britain. If not that, then a celebrity chef. And Meg really should be a supermodel. Yet I sometimes feel as if I'm holding them back, by expecting them to do all this for me to the detriment of their own careers. I can't even pay them.'

'Sometimes people only want what they already have. Good friends, a roof over their heads and love. The latter being the most important thing. Regardless of what you want for your friends, they don't need to chase any other dream, because they're already living a dream. Anyone can see that.'

'Yes, it must be nice to find that kind of love. One that fulfils all your needs.'

Matt stiffened. 'You speak as if you'll never find it.'

'I . . . I don't know. I just wish things weren't so complicated.'

'Then we'll just have to un-complicate them.'

'How do we do that?'

Before Matt could answer, they heard a cry from the hall, which sounded like 'Bon Dieu'.

'Philly!' Meg ran into the room. It was supposed to be a scene where, Meg, now acting as one of the other teachers, came in to tell them that Dominique couldn't be found any-where. This made what she actually said all the more surprising. 'Monsieur De Lacey has fallen down the stairs.'

'What?' It took Philly a moment to realise it was not a part of the performance.

Philly, Matt and Puck rushed to the hallway, closely followed by curious guests.

De Lacey was sitting awkwardly at the bottom of the stairs. 'I tripped on the carpet runner,' he explained, his face flushed with pain. 'My ankle, I think it's broken.'

'Let me see,' said Puck. When De Lacey looked unsure, Puck said, 'Don't worry, I'm the First Aider here. I know what I'm doing.' It was a requirement of running the weekends that they had someone qualified on the premises.

'It's certainly badly bruised,' said Puck after he had examined De Lacey's foot. 'I can't feel any breakages. Still, we'd best get you to the hospital for an X-ray. Matt, can you drive us there, whilst I take care of Monsieur De Lacey?'

There was no real reason for Matt to drive — Monsieur De Lacey was not in any mortal danger after all. Philly got the distinct impression from the look her friend gave her that Puck was taking Matt with him so that she and Meg wouldn't have to worry about keeping an eye on the attic area whilst they were out of the house. Or at least, not have to worry that Matt was going to search through it, whilst they were busy elsewhere.

For his part, Matt didn't appear to see anything strange in the request. 'Sure, no problem.'

Philly watched from the door as the three men drove away. Meg stood next to her, and put her hand on Philly's shoulder. 'It'll be all right, love, don't worry.'

'I hate to sound selfish,' said Philly, 'and I really do hope Monsieur De Lacey is okay, but what if he sues, Meg? He said the runner was loose. It'll break us completely.'

Philly and Meg walked back to the stairs, where the group of guests were already examining the scene of the crime. One might easily have come to the conclusion that this event was more exciting to them than the pretend drama of Dominique's disappearance.

'There's no loose runner that I can see,' said Mr Graham. The other guests murmured in agreement. The old man took a digital camera from his pocket. 'I'll get evidence for you,' he added, patting Philly on the shoulder kindly. 'If you ask me, lass, the mon-sewer didn't want to admit he had a bit too much of the falling-down water last night.'

11

'Try not to worry too much,' said Mrs Cunningham, patting Philly's arm. 'I'm sure Monsieur De Lacey will be fine.'

'I hope so,' she replied.

Philly and Meg had somehow managed to improvise the next piece of the fictional drama before Philly took a group to the kitchen to prepare lunch. The Saturday lunch group were making pizzas, with much hilarity ensuing as they tried to spin thick wads of dough on their hands.

Philly, Puck and Meg had arranged most of the meals accordingly, so that the guests had fun preparing the food rather than thinking they were being forced to supply their own meals.

Only Saturday evening's dinner would be a little less complicated, as it was a traditional Christmas meal, complete with turkey and roast pork, with an alternative of spinach and goats' cheese tartlets for the vegetarians in the group.

Puck had left instructions to be sure that the turkey crowns and pork loins were put in the oven in plenty of time. Thankfully all the guests in that rota had to do was prepare the vegetables, roll bacon around sausages, make the bread sauce and put the Christmas puddings on to steam.

'Everyone could see it was an unfortunate accident,' said Mrs Cunningham. She was busy chopping tomatoes and mushrooms for the pizza toppings, whilst Philly grated a block of cheese. 'I don't know if the good man was drunk or hungover, but I don't think your carpet runner had anything to do with it.'

'I feel really selfish, worrying about that,' said Philly.

'But you're not a selfish girl, anyone can see that.'

'That's very kind. Thank you.'

'Oh, this really takes me back,' said

Mrs Cunningham. 'Not the kitchen duties. They weren't in my remit. But being in this house. It's amazing the things you remember. School assemblies — they were in the ballroom, of course, it being the largest room in the house. The chatter of the girls. I can almost hear it. Even the night time walking about.'

'Did you sleep here? I thought you lived in the vicarage.'

'I did live in the vicarage. But it was part of my contract that I spent at least one night a week here, to give other teachers a night off from having to listen out for the girls.'

'Were you here the night Dominique went missing?'

'Erm . . . ' Mrs Cunningham thought about it for a moment. 'Actually, no. I came into work the next morning — I was a bit late because I had a doctor's appointment — that was when I learned I was having our son, Michael.' She smiled at the remembrance. 'Anyway, I found everyone searching for her because she hadn't turned up for assembly, and missed her first lesson. Sometimes girls did, you know, because they wanted to get out of doing a particular class. Usually because they had forgotten to do their homework. So we didn't worry too much at first. Only as the day wore on, and there was no sign of her did we call the police in. One thing you could be sure of with Dominique was that she turned up for meal times.'

Philly lowered her voice a little. 'I can't remember where I heard it, but someone mentioned that a young lad called Harry was arrested here around that time.'

'Oh yes. I'd almost forgotten about that. Harry . . . erm.' Mrs Cunningham frowned. 'Oh, I would pick now to have a senior moment, wouldn't I? I forget his surname. He was found with money on him and claimed some man and woman had willingly given it to him.'

'Was it when Dominique went missing?'

'Let me think. Yes, it was near that time. But not the same night, obviously, otherwise I'm sure the police would have connected it.'

'You don't think Dominique might have been involved with Harry, then?'

'I doubt it. As I've already told you, she was a girl without grace. Not that it's entirely impossible. But I'm pretty sure Harry was locked up when Dominique went missing. Not only that, but he was a bit younger than her, if I remember rightly. Oh, what was his surname?'

'I heard,' said Philly, lowering her voice even further to be sure that no one else heard, 'that Mrs Bennett was his sister. Irene. Does that ring a bell?'

'Oh yes, now you come to mention it. I remember her too. Such a sweet little girl. Their parents owned the local shop. But Harry was a bad lot. Left home at fourteen, not long after being arrested here, and was nothing but trouble for them. I wonder what happened to him?'

'He went to Australia and became a successful businessman, according to Mrs Bennett;' Philly replied.

'Really? How wonderful. That is good to know. I don't think he has anything to do with Dominique's disappearance. Let me ponder on it for a while and see what else I can remember. Being here has been a great help to me. Seeing the rooms, and soaking up the atmosphere. It seems that this house has never changed. It has a way of . . . '

'Of what?' asked Philly, even though she already knew what the older woman was going to say.

'Inspiring devotion, even to those who don't live here, but merely come here to work. It's almost as if it's a living, breathing creature. But it's a hungry creature, too. It's always hungry.'

'What do you mean by that?' asked Philly.

'Oh, you must know, dear. It soaks up money like a sponge. When it was rented out to the school, the agreement was that we were responsible for the upkeep during our tenure. It cost a fortune to keep the roof fixed. It was always raining or snowing in somewhere. Then there was the heating bill.'

'Tell me about it,' groaned Philly. 'We just run around a lot when we don't have guests.'

'I'm sure your godmother meant well in leaving it to you, but it's a big burden for a young woman. The occasional murder mystery weekends are a wonderful idea, but . . . well I hope you don't mind me saying this, they won't help in the end. The older the house gets, the more you'll have to do to it. And it's quite ancient in places now.'

Philly wouldn't have felt comfortable discussing such things with other guests, but she had come to think of Mrs Cunningham as a friend.

'I know. And because it's a Grade II listed building, it generally costs more. That's if we can even find the artisans with the skills to keep it maintained.' Philly smiled sadly. 'You talk of being devoted to the house, and I am. But sometimes I think I hate it too. Oh, listen to me. I'm sure that's only as a result of Monsieur De Lacey's fall.'

'I don't think that's all, dear. The talk amongst the guests is that there's something going on between the headmaster and the games mistress. They all think it's part of the play, but I'm not so sure. I think you have doubts.'

Philly nodded. 'I just don't think that I'm ready for a relationship, with everything I have to do here.'

'I don't think that's it either, but I shan't press you for details. At least not with people in listening distance. Remember that if you ever need a friend, you can talk to me. Young people sometimes think us wrinklies know nothing of love and sex. But the truth is, you didn't invent it in the twenty-first century. We discovered it in the 1950s.'

'I thought Philip Larkin said it was invented in 1963,' she answered, laughing.

'Oh, he was a few years out, that's all. But as an ex-English teacher I am glad to hear you know your Larkin!'

★ ★ ★

The men arrived back during lunch. Philly went into the hall to meet them, having only managed to chew a morsel of pizza.

Monsieur De Lacey had a crutch. 'Nothing is broken, as your good friend Puck said earlier,' he said, taking Philly's hand in his. 'Mademoiselle, I am desolated to think that you blame yourself for this. I am a clumsy old man, and it was entirely my fault. Monsieur Puck, Monsieur Matt, thank you for helping me. Now I am hungry, and I think I smell pizza, yes?'

'Are you staying?' asked Philly. 'You're very welcome to, of course. I just thought that after this you might prefer to leave. We don't have a lift, unfortunately.'

'Please, do not fret. I am able to take

the stairs one at a time, and I would not want to miss my Christmas dinner.'

'We've saved you all some pizza,' said Philly, relief sweeping through her. 'I promise that not too much of the dough was dropped on the floor.'

'That's very comforting,' said Matt, reaching down and kissing her cheek. Yet she couldn't help noticing that Matt and Puck exchanged serious glances.

There was no time to ask them what was wrong, so she simply led them to the dining room, where Monsieur De Lacey's return was greeted with happy cries of welcome from the other guests. He may not have broken his foot, but his fall went a long way to breaking any remaining ice amongst the guests, giving them something to discuss over their meal.

The rest of the afternoon was taken up with more improvised drama, as the hosts and assembled guests worked their way through several different motives for Dominique's disappearance.

The guests seemed to be thinking in terms of Russian spies, and the race for space. It did cross Philly's mind to wonder why such spies — and a French one at that — would be in a British boarding school, when the race was clearly between Americans and Russians. However, Matt's presence did add some authenticity to the idea, so she didn't argue. He was handsome enough to be an astronaut, though why he would be working as a headmaster was less plausible.

'Maybe I'm CIA,' he said, when Philly mentioned her misgivings to him. She had a strange desire to make the solution plausible.

'Yeah, that works. But why here?'

'I don't know. Maybe I just followed my heart.'

'Hmm. And just happened to be where you needed to be when there was international intrigue.'

'Hey, if it works for Bruce Willis, it works for me.'

'Do you own a white vest?' said Philly

with a grin. 'Because we're not doing this plot if you don't.'

'Of course I own a white vest. It's required of all American heroes. In fact, I'm pretty sure it's written in the constitution.'

The panic of the morning had subsided, as Monsieur De Lacey happily joined in again, albeit from the comfort of whatever armchair was handy. He seemed to be enjoying himself, not least because a few of the ladies took it upon themselves to pander to his every whim, bringing him coffee and other drinks when he requested them. And sometimes, it seemed, even before he thought of it himself.

The Bennetts and Mr Graham treated it with amusement, as did the Cunninghams. Only Stan Scattergood harrumphed and complained about the bourgeoisie.

'I bet he's jealous because he's not being waited on hand and foot,' said Meg, whilst the four friends were in the kitchen, making afternoon tea.

'He's certainly milking it,' said Puck, who seemed, unusually for him, to be in a bad mood.

'You can say that again,' said Matt.

'Are you two all right?' Philly asked them. 'You've both been a bit quiet since you got back from the hospital.'

'Yeah, we're fine,' said Puck. 'It's just that . . . well, we don't think De Lacey fell down the stairs.'

'But he's got bruises, hasn't he?'

'Oh yeah, they're there. But . . . well, I'm not an expert at First Aid, not having had a chance to use my skills, but Matt had misgivings. Perhaps you should tell them, Matt.'

'I'm not much of an expert either,' said Matt, 'but it seemed to me that the bruises weren't new. They're recent, but they came up far too quickly from the time he fell down the stairs. We wondered if De Lacey hurt himself elsewhere, before coming here, and decided to try to blame you.'

'So he could sue me, you mean?'

'Maybe.'

'But he said in front of everyone that it wasn't my fault. That's a bit silly if he's trying to get a fortune out of me.'

'I don't know.' Matt shrugged. 'Perhaps he realised that we guessed what he was up to, so he changed his mind.'

'We're wasting our time on the Dominique thing,' Meg said. 'Maybe we should be investigating the mystery of Monsieur De Lacey's foot.'

'I'm guessing the butler did it,' declared Puck.

'I think it's more likely Mr Scatter-good,' countered Philly. 'They don't like each other very much.'

When they had finished preparing the tea, Matt picked up the tray of tea things and left the kitchen. Philly was just about to follow him with the plate of cakes, when Puck stopped her.

'About Matt,' he said.

'What about him?' said Philly, fearing that Puck had found out something she'd prefer not to know.

'Nothing. That's just it. He seems a straight-up bloke and a good friend. Last night when we were searching the attic, he was genuinely furious that you'd been frightened so badly. I was half afraid that if we did find someone, Matt would punch the guy's lights out. I can't work it out, Philly. I can't work him out.'

'But I heard . . . '

'I know, sweetheart, but now I'm wondering whether you misunderstood what was said.'

'It was pretty clear, Puck.'

'Then there must be some other explanation. If there isn't, I can't help thinking that it takes a very dangerous man to have fooled us all in the way he has.' Puck sighed. 'Sorry, I meant to set your mind at rest, but it doesn't look as if I have.'

'Let's just get this weekend over,' said Philly. 'Then I'll worry about Matt.' If her friends couldn't even make up their minds whether he was a bad guy or not, she fretted, what hope did she have of coming to a decision?

As she walked to the drawing room with the tea cakes, she began to look forward to the weekend being over, and having the house to herself again. Or at least to herself, Puck and Meg. Opening her house up to paying guests was fine for helping to pay the bills, but not so good for her nerves.

As well as Monsieur De Lacey's fall, there were a dozen other things to worry about, along with the minor complaints and requests that the guests had, such as the loo in their en suite not flushing properly or simply wanting extra tea bags and milk for their rooms. It would be easier if she could employ chambermaids to help with cleaning the rooms and changing the bedding, but it was left to Philly and her friends.

There barely seemed to be a minute when she had time to stop and think about what was happening, not just with Matt and De Lacey but also with the prowler in the attic. So she slowed down a little, reasoning that being a few seconds late with the cakes wouldn't make a difference.

She felt certain the noise was not just a rat. Someone had unlocked the door and could be heard hunting around in the attic when she and Meg climbed the stairs. If only they hadn't dithered so much! They should have gone straight in there and confronted the person, before they had time to hide.

Where had they gone afterwards? Had they somehow managed to get out of the room whilst Philly, Meg and Matt were on their way downstairs? Perhaps hiding in one of the upper rooms. No, that couldn't be it, as Puck had come from his room and was waiting at the top of the staircase when they went down. He went straight to the attic with the key that Philly secretly handed to him as she passed. As far as she knew there hadn't been a moment when the attic door was unattended, until Puck locked it after he and Matt had searched for the prowler.

So whoever it was must have been

hiding somewhere in there. But where? Matt and Puck had searched, but maybe they didn't search everywhere. After all, the light wasn't very bright, and didn't reach into every corner. There were also many big trunks. It was possible the prowler hid in one of those.

Reaching the drawing room, Philly put the plate of cakes down. 'Help yourself,' she said, rather more brusquely than she intended. 'If you'll excuse me I need to . . . erm . . . yes. Sorry.'

Let them think she desperately wanted the loo, she thought as she dashed out of the room. What she really wanted to do was get a look in the attic. Darkness would be falling soon, and she didn't like the idea of going up there late at night. Not least because she didn't fancy encountering another warm, furry rat.

There was something spooky about the attic, even in daytime. It hadn't always felt like it, but due to the events of the night before, Philly felt the hairs on the back of her neck prickle as she unlocked the door. Of course, no one could be in there now — unless the intruder had spent the night locked in. It was doubtful. All the guests had been at lunch, apart from Monsieur De Lacey, who had been at the hospital with Puck and Matt. The only alternative was that a stranger had come into the house, which didn't bear thinking about.

Philly grinned to herself. 'Of course,' she muttered, wryly. 'It's so much worse for the intruder to be from outside, rather than be someone sleeping under my own roof.' On the other hand, it was better. Because it would mean it wasn't Matt.

She wondered if she should have it out with him once the guests had gone. Find out exactly why he wanted to get into the attic. Thinking about it fortified her. It would be much better to get things out in the open, rather than coping with the doubts and fears which assailed her. Even if it did mean definitely getting her heart broken. It might be painful, but anything had to be better than the limbo in which she existed at the moment. At least then it would be at an end, and she could get on with getting over him.

As she went over the options in her mind, one moment thinking she would talk to Matt, and the next shying away from the idea like a frightened kitten, she searched the attic for signs that someone had been up there. It wasn't easy, considering that she had hunted around either on her own or with Puck and Meg. They hadn't exactly been methodical in their search patterns, simply lifting things up and casting them aside.

As Philly passed the dormer window, she felt an icy draught, and drew her arms around herself. Even with a thick sweater on, she was cold. The attic had no heating, having been used for nothing but storage, but normally the heat from the rest of the house rose and kept it pleasantly warm.

Looking closer, she saw that the

dormer window was slightly open. She was sure Matt and Puck said it was fastened tightly. She went to look and opened it wider, looking out. It was then that she realised the window was directly over the kitchen. Stretching out as far as she could, Philly looked down and saw a clear patch of roof where the snow had slid down onto the ground below. But the rest of the snow was still on the roof and had clearly not thawed, as Puck suggested.

Looking to either side, Philly saw that on the left hand side of the window, there were long ridges in the snow, where someone had obviously been perching outside the window.

12

'Philly? Philly, where are you?' Matt's voice called up from one of the lower floors.

'I'll be down in a minute.' Philly closed the window and fastened it tightly. As she turned, she was sure that she saw a thin stream of light coming from somewhere in the corner of the attic. She hadn't noticed it before, and she was eager to investigate. Matt's presence stopped her. It would be much better to check it out when she was alone, in case it was something to do with him wanting to get into the attic.

'We need the key to the wine cellar,' said Matt, much closer than she imagined. He stood resting against the attic doorframe. 'What are you doing up here?'

'Someone was on the roof,' she said,

feeling that there was no harm in telling him that much. 'That's what dislodged the snow. They left the window open slightly.'

'That's impossible. It was fastened when Puck and I checked last night.'

'Then they must have hidden somewhere until you'd gone.' Philly was about to tell him about the stream of light, but again decided to keep it a secret. Until she knew what she was dealing with, she would only share things with Matt that he already knew about. 'In one of the trunks, maybe.'

'We checked everything. Do you doubt me, Philly?'

Now that was a question and a half, thought Philly. Where to begin with answering it . . .

'I'd better come and see to the wine, I suppose. We'll talk about it later when the guests are settled down for the evening.'

'Okay, but I want an answer to that question eventually.'

Ignoring him, Philly locked the attic

door and put the key in her pocket. She couldn't help noticing that he watched her the whole time. She made a promise to herself to hide the key somewhere else as soon as she had the chance. Meanwhile an idea was forming. Something that would prevent anyone from prowling around the house for at least half of Saturday night going into Sunday morning.

'How is the drama going?' she asked Matt, as they walked down the stairs.

'Fine. Meg and Puck in their respective roles have had the big argument over Dominique's disappearance. So the guests have decided I'm not in the CIA, but that there is some sort of criminal activity going on at Bedlington Hall involving the teachers. They think Dominique was silenced when she unearthed their criminal scheme. Pity — I really did want to be in the CIA.'

'I hope Mrs Cunningham is not offended.'

'No, she thinks it's highly amusing.'

'It does make me wonder, though . . .'

'What?' Matt paused on the lower staircase, waiting for Philly to catch up with him.

'Maybe there *was* something criminal going on. Why else would a man and woman in the grounds at night pay Harry off?'

'If he was telling the truth. A petty thief, and a fourteen-year-old one, is not the most reliable of witnesses.'

'Exactly,' said Philly. 'This makes it more likely that it's true.'

'There's logic in that, Jim, but not as we know it,' Matt said in his best *Star Trek* voice.

Philly would have responded, but Mr and Mrs Bennett had started up the stairs.

'Are you both all right?' Philly asked in concern.

'Oh yes, love,' said Mrs Bennett. 'We're just going to have a nap before dinner, if you don't mind.'

'Of course we don't. We want you to be comfortable.'

'We didn't get much sleep last night, with all the excitement,' said Mr Bennett.

'Oh, I am sorry,' said Philly sincerely. 'I didn't mean to disturb everyone.'

'Don't worry,' said Mrs Bennett. 'It was exciting really. If you hadn't had that rule about only doing the drama bits downstairs, I'd have thought it was part of the act. You ought to bear it in mind for your next one. Besides, it wasn't you, dear. Someone near to us broke a glass. Then there was some bumping around. We know you didn't mean to disturb anyone, but some people have no consideration, do they?'

'No, they don't, but I am sorry,' said Philly. 'I'll tell you what, I'll give you a bit of a refund. How does fifty pounds sound?'

'Oh, no that's . . . ' Mrs Bennett started to say, before her husband interrupted.

'That'll be grand, lass, thank you,' he said. 'It'll make up for the draught as well.'

'The draught?'

'Yes, coming from the room next to ours. There's an adjoining door, you see, and I suppose it's because there's no heating on in there.'

Philly remembered then that Rooms One and Two were indeed connected, having once been a gentleman's bedroom and dressing room. The door was always kept locked, and she had considered blocking off the door, but changed her mind in case they ever decided to open up the house to family groups.

'Actually the heating system works in all the rooms on that floor,' said Philly. 'But maybe the radiator needs bleeding or something. I'll check it before bedtime so you don't have another night's unrest. But I have to see to the wine now, so if you could just put up with it a little while longer . . .'

'You're a good girl,' said Mrs Bennett, tapping Philly on the arm. 'We'll put a blanket against the gap for now, shall we?'

'Yes, that's a good idea. And if you're cold there are more blankets in the closet opposite your room. I think there are some hot water bottles in there too, so do make use of them.'

'Philly,' said Matt, when the Bennetts had gone upstairs. 'You can't keep giving money away like that, sweetheart.'

'But if they're unhappy with the house, Matt, I have to put things right.'

'They didn't say they were unhappy. They just told you what happened. I'm sure they had no thoughts of getting a refund until you mentioned it.' He reached up and stroked her cheek. 'I just don't want to see you conned, that's all, darling.'

'Don't you?' said Philly, feeling as if she might cry at any minute. If he didn't want to see her conned, what was he doing there? His interest in the attic was every bit as strong as the other intruders. Philly felt unsafe in her own home, and as much as she wanted to trust that Matt would care for her and

229

keep her safe, she truly believed that the only people she could trust were herself, Puck and Meg.

'Philly,' said Meg, rounding the corner of the stairs, looking harassed. 'The wine cellar key, sweetheart . . . '

★   ★   ★

Dinner was a suitably festive affair, with everyone getting into the Christmas spirit.

The food was plentiful, and tasted wonderful. Afterwards they all sang carols in the ballroom, where it turned out that Matt played the piano very well. If he was a conman, he was a very talented one. However, when he started to play a medley of 1950s jazz, it did increase Philly's fears that he was just a little bit too good to be true.

Philly and Meg had arranged small presents for everyone. Nothing fancy, just pamper sets for the ladies and shaving foam and aftershave for the men. Not having expected presents at all, the guests were delighted, especially when Puck dressed up as Santa to hand them out.

Soon a queue of women were lining up to sit on his knee and whisper their Christmas wishes to him. Judging by the embarrassed expression on his face and the way his eyes widened from time to time, some were a little on the risque side.

'I think they all want Santa in their stocking,' Meg whispered to Philly, causing both to fall into a fit of giggles.

'For goodness' sake, go and rescue him, Meg,' Philly chuckled. 'The poor boy looks terrified.'

'Nah, I'll let him suffer a bit more,' said Meg, winking. 'It's good for his soul.'

'I wish we'd known about this,' said Mrs Cunningham, kissing Philly and Meg on the cheek. 'We'd have brought you something. Andrew and I will be sure to treat you when it's really Christmas.'

'Oh no, there's no need for that,' said

Philly. 'Really. It just seemed strange to have a Christmas party and not give out presents. And I've had a great idea for later on tonight.'

'What's that?' asked Mrs Cunningham.

Philly had meant to keep it a complete secret, but as she considered Mrs Cunningham a friend, she was eager to tell her. 'A midnight feast! We've got so much food left over, and once we've had everyone dancing for a while, they're sure to be hungry again.'

'How wonderful! You must let me help.'

'That would be great, thank you. We're going to hold it in one of the spare bedrooms upstairs. That way if anyone is tired, their own room will be a sanctuary. But don't tell the others yet,' Philly urged. 'I want it to be a surprise. In fact, I've pushed a note under everyone's door, which they should get when they go up to bed. It says Midnight Feast, Room One.'

She'd already decided to do the

midnight feast, in an attempt to put off prowlers and intruders, but hadn't worked out where. The Bennetts complaint had reminded her that Room One was not only empty but also directly opposite the junction of the staircase. She hadn't put guests in it, due to its proximity to both staircases. It made it rather noisy late in the evening as everyone was making their way to bed.

During the feast, she could leave the door open and keep an eye on the stairs, for at least part of the night. That was if anyone was foolish enough to try the attic again. She half-hoped, half-dreaded they would.

As Philly thought of her plans, the piano fell silent, and Matt went to the music system, flicking a switch. The ballroom was filled with the sound of 1960s rock 'n' roll; the music having been chosen especially to reflect the era in which the drama took place. As most of the guests were of that age, they smiled delightedly and were soon jigging around the room.

'Oh, do you remember this, Frank?' asked Mrs Bennett, grabbing her husband's hand.

'How could I? I'm too young,' he replied, grinning. Nevertheless, he danced happily with his wife, whilst their friend, Mr Graham, took a turn with another lady. She had come to the weekend alone too, and it seemed they were getting on very well indeed.

'An autumn love affair,' said Mrs Cunningham, smiling in their direction. 'How wonderful.'

Reverend Cunningham came over and took his wife's hand and they showed that they also knew a few moves.

Everyone seemed to be having a good time, except Stan Scattergood, who sat in the corner alone. He had not gelled well with the rest of the guests, seeming to set himself apart from them. Even though Philly didn't like him very much either, as the hostess she felt she ought to make a little more effort with him.

He was hard work though, so she made a mental note not to beat herself up too much if she failed to bring him out of himself.

'Would you like to dance, Mr Scattergood?' she asked.

'I would not.'

'Okay — well is there anything I can get you? A drink? Some more food?'

'I'm perfectly happy here, alone.' Scattergood emphasised the last word, making it clear he saw Philly's presence as an intrusion into his personal space.

Not one to give up so easily, Philly sat down opposite him. 'I'm sorry you're not happy, Mr Scattergood. I don't mean to be rude, but it makes me wonder why you came. This is obviously not your sort of weekend.'

'No, you're right, it isn't. All these idiots playing at being sleuths. Most people don't see what's right under their nose.'

Philly followed the direction of his eyes to the dance floor, wondering who he was talking about.

'So why did you come?'

'A whimsy, I suppose. Wanting to relive an old life. Now I realise you can't go back. Not really.'

'An old life? You've been here before?'

'Ay, a long time ago. You're like her, you know. Same pretty blue eyes.'

'Sorry? Like who?'

'Robyn Sanderson.'

'You knew my godmother? Why didn't you say?'

'Because you didn't need to know. It's not as if me and you are anything to do with each other.'

She had to give Mr Scattergood his due. He was honest, albeit brutally so. 'Well, no, but I'm always happy to meet her friends. I didn't know any of them, you see. It was as if . . . Oh, I don't know. As if Aunt Robyn had a separate life to the one she occasionally shared with me. I was at boarding school most of the time. When I was with her, it really was just us. So do tell me about her, please. I mean, if you don't mind.'

Mr Scattergood visibly relaxed. 'Like I said, you're a lot like her. She always wanted to include people. Be everyone's friend. Bit silly, sometimes, but there you are. That's why it was so hard for her, I suppose.'

'What was hard for her?'

'She changed after you came along. Settled down a bit. She said she didn't want to live the old life. That included seeing her old friends. Bit tough on us.' Mr Scattergood took a drink from his wine glass. He hadn't really answered Philly's question.

'Yes, I realise it must have been hard for her, suddenly stuck with a child to care for. I'm sorry if you resented my appearance on the scene. Did . . . I know this is a rude question, but did you love her?'

'We all did. It was impossible not to. Look, I'm not blaming you. She did what she had to do, and she never regretted it. I just wish she'd let us in a bit. We might even have been able to help her. Not that she wanted our type of help,' he added.

'What do you mean, your type of help? I don't understand.'

'Nothing. Let it go now. It's in the past. Don't pay too much attention to a miserable old goat like me, Philomela.'

'You really did know my godmother, didn't you? No one else here knows my full name.'

'It means nightingale, doesn't it?'

'Yes, that's right.'

'So can you sing, Miss Nightingale?'

'Actually I can.'

'Do you know that old French song? I can never remember the French version. I think Edith Piaf sang it. Something about no regrets.'

'*Non, je ne regrette rien*? Yes, Aunt Robyn taught it to me.'

'Ah, that's the one. It was her theme tune, that song. Robyn always said she would regret nothing, and I don't think she ever did. You asked what would make me happy. It'll make me happy to hear you sing that.'

'Okay,' said Philly. 'Erm . . . perhaps

tomorrow, because everyone is dancing now.'

'You're not getting out of it that easily, Philly,' said a voice behind her. She hadn't realised Matt was listening. 'I know the tune. It's one of my mom's favourites. Your wish is our command, Mr Scattergood.'

Before she could argue, Matt had switched off the music. 'Ladies and gentlemen,' he said, tapping on a glass to get their attention. 'It seems we have a songstress in our midst. Please put your hands together for Miss Philomela Sanderson.'

'I'll get you for this,' Philly said through gritted teeth as she followed Matt to the piano. She hated her full name and tried never to use it.

'Hey,' he said, as he sat down. 'If Mr Scattergood ends the evening with a smile on his face, you'll be thanking me.'

'I don't mean that. I mean for telling everyone my full name.'

'It's a beautiful name, for a beautiful

girl. Are you ready?'

'No.'

'Good, then we'll start.' Matt began to play the opening bars of the song.

Despite her misgivings, as soon as Philomela heard it, she wanted to sing. Music had always had that effect on her. She didn't sing to the standard heard in the West End, as many a director had told her during auditions for shows, but she did have a pretty enough singing voice. Luckily the song was one of those where, even if people didn't think they knew it, as soon as they heard the tune, they recognised it. She sang it once in French, then in English, much to the delight of the guests.

When she had finished, there was a rapturous round of applause and calls for an encore from the guests. Philly refused gracefully. The song had stirred up disturbing emotions in her, remembering her godmother, and the few precious moments they shared together.

As if Matt understood, he started playing one of the livelier songs from

Oliver, gesturing Puck, who had taken off the Santa suit, to join him in a rousing chorus of *Consider Yourself*.

Philly looked across to Mr Scattergood. He wasn't exactly smiling, but he was wiping his eyes with a white handkerchief. He looked back at Philly and raised a thumb, still not smiling, but nodding. She'd made him content, but in a very emotional way.

Scanning the room, to watch everyone join in the song playing, Philly saw Mrs Cunningham standing in a corner with her husband. She seemed pensive again, involved in a discussion with her husband that clearly disturbed them both. He tenderly stroked his wife's hair, and although Philly was not much of a lip reader, she sensed he was saying, 'Try not to worry about it, darling.'

★   ★   ★

It was an hour later that Philly, Meg and Mrs Cunningham went upstairs to sort out Room One ready for the midnight feast.

'Are you all right, Mrs Cunningham?' asked Meg when they were at the top of the stairs. 'You seem tired. Are you sure you want to do this?'

'What? Oh yes, dear. I'm fine. I just don't have the energy I used to have. But I think Philly's idea is wonderful.'

'Well, if it gets too much for you,' said Philly, 'you let me know. There isn't much we need to do. I want to check the radiator mostly, make sure it's not too cold in there.'

Philly opened the door and went in, to be met by a severe blast of air coming from the window. The curtains were drawn, but blowing open. Flicking on the light switch, she took a few steps forward.

'Careful!' said Mrs Cunningham, grabbing her arm.

Philly stopped short. On the floor in front of the window was a pile of broken glass.

13

'It's impossible,' said Philly, sweeping the broken glass into a dustpan. She had quickly explained to Mrs Cunningham what had really happened on the previous night in the attic. 'Climbing down there would be deadly. Especially in the snow.'

As well as the broken glass, a row of dirty footprints stained the carpet near to the window.

'I thought I heard glass breaking in the night,' said Meg. 'I suppose I assumed someone had dropped a bedside glass.'

'I heard it too,' said Philly. 'So did Mr and Mrs Bennett. Whoever it was must have climbed down, then broken the window here to open the latch. But the attic window is at the back of the house. They'd have had to go up over the roof first. It's a wonder they didn't kill themselves.'

'The only other explanation would be ice falling from the roof and blowing into the window,' said Mrs Cunningham. 'However, that doesn't explain the footprints, does it?'

'No, it doesn't.' Philly put the dustpan on the bedside table for a moment and rubbed her forehead. A headache began to form behind her eyes, and she longed again for an empty house and the solitude of her own bedroom. 'I still don't understand how whoever it was managed to hide from Matt and Puck. Unless they were in one of the trunks.'

'That seems the most plausible explanation,' said Mrs Cunningham. 'Who do you suspect?'

Philly and Meg exchanged glances. 'Well . . . it doesn't really matter who we suspect because we were wrong,' said Philly, wondering whether to elaborate. 'He was downstairs all along.'

'And who is this mysterious man?' asked Mrs Cunningham. 'Come along, dear, narrow it down for me a little.'

Philly went over and shut the door, in case of eavesdroppers. Then she went over to sit on the bed with Meg and Mrs Cunningham.

'A few weeks ago, I overheard Matt telling someone on the phone that he wanted to get into the attic.'

'Matt?' exclaimed Mrs Cunningham. 'Matt Cassell? But Philly, I thought you and he were . . . well, involved, as the young call it nowadays.'

'I don't know what we are,' she replied, sadly. 'I wanted to trust him but it's so hard, knowing what I know. We were going to set a trap for him, you see. That's how I came to lose the key to the attic in the first place. Normally it's hung up with all the other keys.'

'But he seems such a nice, genuine young man and you make a lovely couple.'

At that, a tear rolled down Philly's cheek.

'Oh don't, love,' said Meg, putting her arm around her friend. 'I know you're hurt, but if he's conning you, he's not worth it.'

'Yes, but even you and Puck say he seems straight-up,' said Philly. 'I don't know what to believe.'

'I tend to follow my heart in these situations,' said Mrs Cunningham, patting Philly on the shoulder. 'What does your heart tell you?'

'I don't know. It seems to change its mind rather a lot. One moment I want to trust him, because he's so lovely to me, and to everyone else, then I remember what I overheard and I'm not sure about him any more. I can't decide if I'm dancing on air or wading through treacle half the time. I do know he wants to get into the attic, and it doesn't matter how many times I've played that phone conversation back in my head, it still comes out the same way.'

'Yes,' said Meg, 'and we let him get into the attic last night. All right, he was with Puck, but it was an excuse for him to have a look around.'

'Hmm ... ' Mrs Cunningham

murmured. 'There is certainly something strange going on here, that's for sure.'

'Mrs Cunningham, please don't take this the wrong way,' said Philly, 'but is it at all possible anyone at the school was engaged in criminal activity? I don't mean you, of course.'

'Why not me?' Mrs Cunningham smiled. 'If you're going to suspect that handsome young man downstairs, why not a doddery old woman?'

'You're anything but doddery!'

'And you're too kind, dear. But in answer to your question, I wasn't aware of anything going on at the time. Oh, we'd get the occasional prowler around the place at night. Usually young men from the village, wanting to tempt the girls out to play. There were rumours that during rationing the cook had something going on with the butcher, but that was well before my time. And of course there was the night Harry was arrested.'

Mrs Cunningham paused. Philly and

Meg waited, sensing that Mrs Cunningham hadn't finished yet.

'It's been a strange experience, being here again. I know I've already told you that. All the things I suddenly remember about my time here at the school. But that's not the strangest thing. I've had a distinct sense all weekend that Dominique is among us, trying to send us a message . . . '

'A ghost, you mean?' said Meg, looking alarmed.

'No. Well, yes, actually. But not in the 'ghosties and ghoulies and long-leggedy beasties' sense. More like a telepathic presence. Just last night, Meg, when you spoke in the French accent, I was struck by how awful it was. I'm sorry, dear, I don't mean to be unkind. You're a lovely girl.'

'I'm not offended,' said Meg. 'I know it was rubbish.'

'You did your best.' Mrs Cunningham reached out and patted Meg's knee. 'And it did give us all a giggle. But it was also helpful to me, because it made me realise something I'd never realised at the time. I think having Monsieur De Lacey here helped make up my mind.'

'About what?' asked Philly.

'It was about Dominique's accent. It had never occurred to me at the time. Our discussions were rare, although we occasionally discussed books we'd both read. I suppose I wasn't really taking much notice then. Not to mention the fact that no one was very well travelled in those days, and we didn't get all these foreign stations on television. We didn't get to hear many French accents. What I'm trying to say is that Dominique's accent was all wrong. Perhaps not as bad as Meg's, but wrong all the same. I see that now.'

'What are you saying exactly?'

'Well, I'm saying that I realise now that Dominique wasn't really French.'

'So maybe she was a spy!' exclaimed Meg.

'Perhaps. I don't know. There was

something else. Something that happened tonight. It gave me an even stronger feeling that Dominique is amongst us.'

'What? Here?' The two girls spoke together, sounding eager.

'When you say amongst us,' said Philly, 'are you suggesting she's one of the guests? But who? Irene Bennett is too young, as are some of the other ladies. There is the woman whom Mr Graham has taken up with. I'd say she's about sixty-five or seventy, so it's a possibility.'

'I don't mean physically amongst us, dear,' said Mrs Cunningham. 'Oh, I'm being silly, I suppose. It's just . . . '

Before Mrs Cunningham could finish, someone knocked on the door. It opened and Matt popped his head in.

'Is this the place for the midnight feast? Puck sent me with the mince pies.'

'Oh . . . I'd completely forgotten why we were here,' said Philly.

'What's happening?' Matt frowned,

and looked towards the dustpan, which still had glass in it. The women had been so busy talking they had forgotten all about it.

'The window was broken,' said Philly. 'It seems that our prowler climbed over the roof and got in through the window.'

Matt shook his head. 'Impossible. Not just impossible. It's crazy in this weather. One wrong step in the snow, and they'd have slipped right off the roof.'

'I know, but it's the only explanation for the broken window. The snow was definitely disturbed outside the attic window. I don't think it slipped off at all. I think it was accidentally kicked off when the intruder climbed out. They came down over the roof, broke this window so they could open the latch, and went out through the door. All the doors in the guests' suites need a key to unlock them from the outside, but can be opened without a key from the inside. Look there are even dirty footprints on the floor.'

Matt examined the area near the window. 'I don't like this,' he said. 'I don't like it one little bit. Honey, isn't it time you brought the police in?'

'To do what? As far as I know, nothing is missing.'

'Someone in the house is up to no good. Or maybe it was all a mistake. I don't know. Maybe they went up to the attic just to be nosey and was too embarrassed to admit to being there after you screamed.'

'And you really think we should bring in the police?' said Philly. Whatever else she had expected Matt to say, that was definitely not it.

'Yes, I do. I worry about you. Who knows what sort of madman, or woman, is skulking around the place at night?'

'I'll call them in the morning,' said Philly, looking Matt squarely in the eye. 'But I'm guessing we just messed up their crime scene. If there is a crime.'

'Just tell them of your concerns.

They'll probably only give you an incident number, but it's something on file if anything worse happens.'

'You seem to know a lot about crime,' said Mrs Cunningham.

'What? Yeah, my family deal in insurance. We know all the police procedures.'

'Of course,' said Philly.

Matt's eyes narrowed, but he didn't say anything.

'We'll have to move rooms for the feast,' said Philly. 'I'll put a sign on the door, redirecting them. It's a pity though, because I wanted to be opposite the stairs.'

'So that's what this is about,' said Matt. 'You want to make sure no one goes upstairs. Well, don't worry about that. If I have to sit at the bottom of the staircase all night to keep you safe, I will.'

It was on Philly's mind to ask who would protect her from him, but she bit her tongue.

'Perhaps Puck could sit with you,' she

suggested instead, merely to get his reaction.

'Nah, he's got enough to do. And so have you and Meg. I'm practically having a free holiday. I might as well earn my keep.'

'You've already done that,' said Philly, trying to be fair. 'You've been a very good host.' It was true. He had been; beyond the call of duty.

'I'll keep watch tonight,' he said, emphatically.

'Wonderful,' said Mrs Cunningham.

'Super,' said Meg.

'Why, thanks.' Matt frowned, not quite trusting their sincerity.

★ ★ ★

The midnight feast turned out to be a rather sorry affair, mainly because the guests were still full from dinner and had drunk rather a lot. Most of them were tired and wanted to go to bed. By the time everyone had left, after spending five or ten minutes just to be polite, the only ones left in the room were Philly, Matt, Puck, Meg and the Reverend and Mrs Cunningham. Naturally the conversation turned to their intruder.

'I agree it is rather odd,' said the Reverend, after they had brought him up to date with everything that had happened. 'I've been thinking about young Harry, you know. Mrs Bennett's brother. They were called Johnson, by the way.'

'Yes, that's it,' agreed Mrs Cunningham. 'Johnson.'

'I remember the night he was arrested. I had to go down and be his responsible adult at the station. His parents had a problem with the bottle, you know.'

'Oh yes, I remember now,' exclaimed his wife. 'Do you know, I'd completely forgotten you going to the station.'

'I remember because it was a couple of days before you found out you were expecting Michael, and I remember thinking later that I hope our child doesn't grow up to be as troubled as young Harry.'

'So it was around the time Dominique disappeared,' said Philly, remembering what Mrs Cunningham had said about the disappearance coinciding with her finding out she was pregnant.

The Reverend nodded. 'Yes, it was indeed. But it wasn't the first time young Harry had been found on school premises. He'd had a couple of warnings about loitering, but they didn't find anything on him on the prior occasions. It was only because he had a rather large amount of cash on him that they arrested him that time.'

'Did you believe him when he said a man and woman had given him the money?' asked Matt.

'I did and I didn't. I sensed he was telling the truth, but I also felt that he was hiding something else. It was almost as if he was telling one small truth in order to hide a very big lie. It's a pity about that boy.'

'Why?' said Philly. 'He turned his life

around and became a big businessman in Australia.'

'Yes, so I'd heard. But I can't see it myself. Harry was amongst a group of youngsters I used to mentor. Troubled kids from bad backgrounds. He didn't have a business brain. Art was his thing. I used to wish he would concentrate more on it, but Harry was about making a fast buck, and art took too much time to perfect, I suppose. Do you remember, Meredith,' said the Reverend, turning to his wife, 'when Harry did that fantastic copy of one of Raphael's Madonna paintings for the church Nativity play?'

'Was that Harry?' asked Mrs Cunningham in surprise.

'Yes.'

'I honestly hadn't realised. You probably told me and I've forgotten about it. Along with too many other things, I'm afraid.'

'You do okay,' said the Reverend, patting her hand. 'Another passion of Harry's was the French Revolution. He was a bit too interested in the machinations of the guillotine for my liking. I suppose all youngsters are fascinated by the macabre.'

Philly opened her mouth to speak, then closed it, afraid she would seem stupid. Could it really be him? A teenage boy who became something of an anti-establishment hero?

Matt was two steps ahead of her. 'Robespierre.'

'What?' said the Reverend and his wife.

'Robespierre,' Philly replied. 'The painting that I took to the auction was by Robespierre. No, it couldn't be. Surely Mrs Bennett would have recognised her own brother in the papers.'

'Not necessarily,' said Mrs Cunningham. 'Irene Johnson, as she was then, was very young at the time. No more than five or six. Her parents died not long after Harry went to Borstal, and she went to live with an aunty. If I remember rightly, Robespierre didn't become prominent until the late sixties, early seventies. It's a long time to go without seeing her brother, and even if she saw Robespierre and thought he looked a bit like Harry, she might not have connected the two.'

'I must admit I didn't,' said the Reverend, stroking his chin. 'That's if Harry *did* become Robespierre. From what I remember, Harry was dark-haired. Robespierre had all that long blond hair, didn't he? Used to cover half his face if I remember rightly. And he spoke in that very affected transatlantic drawl, half-American, and half-English. Nothing like the local accent Harry had. Besides, it would never have occurred to me that Harry would be anything other than a petty thief. An attitude which I realise doesn't say much for me.' The Reverend looked rueful.

'We can't always be blamed for the impression we get of people,' said his wife, putting a comforting arm on his shoulder.

'Irene and Harry have had some

contact, though,' said Puck. 'Because the Bennetts knew that Harry was a millionaire living in Australia.'

'Mrs Bennett's family probably only knew what Harry told them, presumably in a letter,' said Matt. 'It isn't as if they could just hop on a plane and go and check at that time. Flights to Australia weren't as frequent or cheap as they are now. There was no Internet with webcams to keep families connected.'

'Yes,' said Reverend Cunningham, nodding, 'and as the years go on, it becomes harder to get in touch with people again. There are many a time I've thought of telephoning some long lost relative or friend, and each time I give myself excuses for not doing it. What if they don't want to hear from me? What if they don't remember me? Plus that good old excuse of being a little busy at the moment, so maybe some other time . . . '

'I'm sure Harry would remember he had a sister,' said Philly.

'But it's still difficult when you lose touch with someone. Especially if that person wants to lose touch,' said Matt.

'We don't know that Harry was . . . is . . . Robespierre,' said Puck, bringing them back to reality. 'We're just guessing.'

'It seems likely, though he must have been very young at the time,' Philly said.

'He was about fourteen, I think,' said the Reverend. 'So, yes, very young. But who knows what was offered to him for his skills? He might have seen it as a way out of here.'

'I didn't think Robespierre was from Midchester,' said Meg. 'I thought he was from a nearby town.'

'He probably reinvented himself,' said Mrs Cunningham. 'So as not to draw attention to his real beginnings.'

'Yes, that's true.'

'I don't suppose we will ever find out,' said Philly. 'He seems to have disappeared. Robespierre, I mean. He may even be dead by now. From what I can make out he was a man of his time, and might not fit into the modern art world. Though I suppose being a forger wouldn't help.'

'We can find out about Irene Bennett's brother, though,' said Matt. 'We can just ask her.'

'I'm not sure about that.' Philly shook her head. 'Mr Bennett said she didn't want to tell people. It might upset her if we ask. She's a nice lady and I'd hate to cause her any pain.'

'Then we just do a search on the Internet for Harry Johnson in Australia,' Puck said. 'If he's genuinely a businessman, he's bound to turn up somewhere. Businesses need to advertise their wares.'

'I've got a feeling there'll be a lot of Harry Johnsons in Australia,' said Philly. 'It's a very common name. Even if we find him, it doesn't answer the question of who is here searching the attic.'

'Unless it is him,' said Matt. 'Think about it. If he was forging paintings, involved in some sort of art scam, maybe some of the originals are hidden up there.'

'But how could they be?' Mrs Cunningham asked, frowning. 'I've already told Philly. We didn't have the key to the attic. Only the family did, and they lived abroad.'

'Did the Sandersons ever come here for anything, Mrs Cunningham?' asked Philly.

'No. At least not when I was here. I don't think we ever met them. The leasing was done through an agent in London. It always seemed rather sad to me that they worked so hard to keep hold of this house, yet couldn't afford to live here.'

'There are only a few small paintings up in the attic,' said Philly. 'I took the Robespierre to the art dealer, and we've put a few others on the walls. I'm pretty sure they're fake.'

Matt nodded. 'Yes, they are.'

'How on earth do you know that?' asked Philly.

'We deal in insurance, darling. So I have to know if what we're insuring is the real thing.'

'Of course,' said Philly. She still felt there was something else Matt wasn't telling her. Why would he make note of the paintings being fake? Unless it was just professional curiosity. Something he couldn't switch off.

Worn out with talking it all through, and finding they only went around in circles, the group said goodnight. Matt walked Philly to her room.

'You're not really going to sit at the bottom of the stairs all night, are you?' she asked him.

'Why not?'

'It just doesn't seem fair.'

'I'll be fine,' he said. 'I'm not sleeping very well at the moment anyway.'

'Why not?'

'Do you even have to ask?' He pulled her into his arms. 'Every time I close my eyes I see a pair of beautiful blue eyes.'

'Oh, Matt . . . ' Philly stroked his

cheek gently, wondering if now was the right time to tell him that she had overheard his telephone conversation.

'What is it?'

'Please don't sit on the stairs all night.'

'You say that as if you're afraid of something.'

Philly couldn't put her fears into words. If Matt were not trying to con her then he might be hurt by the intruder. If he was trying to con her, he had given himself a legitimate excuse for lurking around. All he had to say if he was caught was that he heard someone in the attic so went up to investigate.

'I am afraid,' she whispered. 'I'm afraid that the truth of all this is something that I won't want to hear and I'm afraid that . . . '

'What, darling? Tell me.'

'Nothing.' She shook her head sadly. 'I'm just tired, that's all. Goodnight.'

'Goodnight. Remember to holler if you need me.'

She needed him then, but until she could trust him, she had no plans to tell him that.

Philly had put her pyjamas on when the idea came to her. The means of finding out the truth had been there all along. The only question was why she hadn't thought of it before.

14

'Are you still here?' Philly asked half an hour later, going to sit next to Matt on the stairs. As far as she knew, he hadn't moved from that spot.

'Yep. I thought you'd gone to bed.'

'I couldn't sleep. There is so much going on in my head, I think it might explode.'

'Yes, mine too.' Matt looked exhausted, and a little sad. His eyes were rimmed with dark lines, and it was obvious he was struggling to stay awake.

'Why don't we go downstairs and get some cocoa? Then we can chat about things,' Philly suggested.

'I'm supposed to be on guard.'

'It's a waste of time, Matt, I don't think anyone is going to come up here tonight. Not after all the fuss of last night.' She took his hand. 'Come on. I make good cocoa.'

'I don't doubt it,' he said, following her down the stairs.

'Does your dad mind you being here?' she asked, as she warmed milk on the stove. 'I'm surprised he can spare you.'

'I'm entitled to time off,' said Matt, a little too defensively. He went into the cupboard for the chocolate biscuits, and it struck Philly that he was not only familiar with the house, but the house was familiar with him in it. She told herself it was a dangerous feeling to have. She couldn't get used to him being there. Even though she wanted so much to be able to.

'So what exactly does the job entail? Insuring art work and all that?' She leaned against the worktop. 'Do you have to value them yourself or do you get someone in?'

'A bit of both. What I mean is that we use valuers, but I also have a degree in art, so I know a fake when I see it.'

'So there are no lost Rembrandts on my walls then?'

'Nope. Sorry. Were you hoping there would be?'

'Obviously,' she retorted. 'Then I wouldn't have to worry about this place any more.'

'Philly, I know your godmother said to keep hold of the place at all costs, but try to remember it's just a house, darling. A pile of bricks.'

'It's my pile of bricks.'

'I understand that. Really I do. But my mom always says that it's people who make a house. And this house would be nothing without you in it. So don't go thinking that it's the other way around. That you'd be nothing without the house.'

'I don't think that, Matt.'

'Are you sure? I see you working yourself to the point of exhaustion here, and I can't help wondering to what lengths you would go to keep it.'

'I wouldn't sell a forged Rembrandt as a real one, if that's what you're thinking.' Philly didn't like the way the conversation was going.

269

'No, of course I don't think that. I . . . oh, I don't know. I just think that your godmother placed a terrible burden upon you.'

'It's only the same burden as she had,' said Philly. 'She used to tell me that her father said the same thing. The house must be kept in the family at all costs. Her great-great grandfather helped build most of it, you know. So it isn't just something they bought. It's something they created with their own hands. I sometimes . . . '

'You sometimes what?'

'Oh, it's silly,' Philly grinned awkwardly. 'I sometimes think I can feel their presence in every brick. They're urging me on, wanting me to succeed.'

'At any cost?'

'What? No, of course not. What are you suggesting, Matt?'

He ran his hands through his hair. 'Nothing, I just . . . '

'You think I've got something to do with what's going on in the attic. Is that it?'

'No, I didn't say that. I just wonder sometimes how much you do know.'

'I don't know anything. Why are you saying this? You're the one who couldn't wait to get in there.'

'Excuse me?'

'Oh, I heard your telephone conversation by the lake. 'Leave it to me,' you said and promised you'd get the key to the attic. I don't know what your game is, or whether you planned to seduce the key out of my hands, but you haven't fooled me as much as you think you have.'

'Philly, darling, it's not what you're thinking.' Matt came towards her, his arms outstretched.

'Don't darling me. And keep your arms to yourself.'

At that point, the pan, obviously in tune with their emotions, boiled over, spilling hot liquid onto the cooker. The aroma of burnt milk filled the kitchen. Philly spun around and turned the ring off. Without thinking, she grabbed the metal pan handle, yelping when it

271

burned her hand.

'Let me see,' said Matt.

'No, I don't want you to help me,' she said, tears streaming down her hot cheeks. 'What I want is for you to leave now. Go away, Matt.'

'No, I'm not going away, until you listen to me. But first let me sort your hand out.' He pulled her to the sink and set the cold tap running. 'Hold your hand under there for a while.'

Again, showing that he knew the house almost as well as Philly did, he went into another cupboard for the First Aid kit. Coming back to her, he said, 'I'm not trying to con you, Philly, whatever you may think. This . . . this whole thing goes back to before we were born.'

'What thing?'

'In the late sixties and early seventies, my dad worked as a claims investigator. It's pretty much what I do now, for our company. He became interested in Robespierre, but could never quite catch the guy. It was an obsession for my dad, I suppose. Anyway, it almost cost him his marriage to my mom.'

'So when you saw the picture, you thought I was connected to Robespierre.'

'I didn't know, darling. I just thought I'd come here and see what I could find out.'

'So you *are* conning me.'

'No.'

'Yes, Matt! Yes, you are. Because you've worked your way into my life and that of my friends, pretending to be our friend, and all along you thought we were crooks.'

'You thought *I* was a crook.'

'With damn good reason! This is my house, remember. I'm meant to be here. You're the . . . the *interloper*.'

'I didn't mean things to happen this way, Philly, I promise.'

'So what did you mean, when you practically threw yourself at me outside the auction house, telling me that I was the most beautiful girl you'd ever seen? What was all that, if it wasn't to lie your way into my house and carry on your father's investigation? That's if you're even telling me the truth about that. I have no good reason to believe you.'

'No, I know you don't. But now it's all out in the open, I'm asking you to trust me. Something is definitely going on here.'

'No. There is nothing going on. My friends and I are not crooks, Matt.'

'I know you're not — but someone is. Someone was up in the attic last night. Someone climbed over the roof and broke the window in Room One.' He touched her shoulder gently. 'I'm afraid for you.'

'I'm afraid for me, too — but I don't think the danger is coming from anyone but you.'

'I'm sorry you think that. Because you have to believe me when I tell you that I would never do anything to hurt you.'

'You've already hurt me. More than anyone else ever could.'

'Forgive me?'

'No. I don't forgive you. I'm tired and my hand hurts. I'm going to bed.'

Philly remembered that she couldn't go to bed, not yet. If she went upstairs, Matt would surely follow her and her plan might be ruined. She went to sit at the kitchen table instead.

Without speaking, Matt refilled the pan with milk and set it going again. A few minutes later he put a cup of hot cocoa in front of Philly, along with a plate of biscuits.

'Here, drink this and you might feel better,' he said. He sounded so gentle and kind, it made Philly feel even worse. He sat down opposite her, perhaps realising that he needed to keep some distance, at least for the moment.

'I told you I was engaged before, right?'

'Yes, so?' Philly was tempted to cover her ears. She wasn't sure she wanted to know about Matt's previous girlfriend.

'Her name was Natalie and I thought I really loved her. She was interested in my work, which is rare. Usually when you tell people you're in insurance they either think you're the mafia or the most boring man in the world.'

'I thought mafia,' said Philly.

'Ouch. Okay. Fair enough. Yet you still invited me to stay in your house?'

'Go on with your story.'

'It turned out she was too interested. She was part of a gang of crooks, intent on stealing expensive works of art. She just used me to get information about our clients and their security systems. I made a vow never to trust a pretty face again. So yes, at first I did wonder if you were up to your ears in crime.'

'Thanks very much.'

'I'll remind you that you thought I was a criminal.'

'And I'll remind you that I had more reason to. You conned your way into my house by pretending you liked me.'

'I didn't pretend I liked you, Philly. And I wasn't the one running around London with a Robespierre painting.'

'I didn't steal it! I found it in the

attic, just as I said I had.'

'I know that now. But that doesn't alter the fact that there is a link between this house and Robespierre. And now, with all the stuff about Harry Johnson, it seems I was right. About that at least. But I was wrong about you and I'm sorry. I'm also very glad.' He reached out to touch her hand, but she moved it away. 'I guess you still don't trust me.'

'I don't know what to think any more, Matt. You're not the person I thought you were,' she said sadly.

'Seeing how you thought I was Michael Corleone, I'm pleased to hear that.'

'No, what I mean is you're not the man who seemed interested in me and my friends, and what we're doing here. Everything you've done has been to make sure you get to stay in this house.'

'Not everything.'

'No?'

'No. It might have been like that at first, but it isn't like that now. Philly, I . . .'

Matt was prevented from saying any more when Joe, the cameraman, walked into the kitchen. 'Ah, I thought I smelled cocoa and chocolate biscuits,' he said.

'You certainly did,' said Matt, smiling. 'You might have got a bit of burnt flesh with that too. Philly is the walking wounded.' He was rewarded with a glare from his hostess.

'Ouch,' said Joe. 'Is there still milk in the pan? No, don't get up. I'll do it.'

'You having trouble sleeping, too?' asked Matt.

'Well, I wasn't but . . . ' Joe started to say, but stopped when Philly imperceptibly shook her head. 'But you know how it is. One little sound and you're wide awake.'

'Did you hear something?' asked Matt. 'Maybe I ought to go take a look.'

'Nah, it was nothing. Just someone in the next room, snoring. Rachel, I think.'

Philly stood up, taking her cocoa with her. 'I'm going to bed.'

'Can we talk first?' asked Matt.

'No.'

As she left the kitchen she heard Joe say to Matt, 'Woman trouble, huh?'

* * *

The next morning, Joe was nowhere to be seen. Philly assumed he'd slept in, due to her disturbing him the night before, but she was eager to see if he'd filmed anything.

Whilst Matt had been sitting at the bottom of the stairs, Philly had gone to Joe's room, which was in her wing, and asked him if he could set up a camera, with an infrared lens, at the junction of the stairs, with enough sweep to see anyone going up or down. Though not sure of the legalities, Joe had decided he was game if Philly didn't mind.

She had looked for the camera when she went back to bed, and not found it, so Joe must have hidden it well. It was only when she was in her own bed that it occurred to her that if Joe were the culprit, he wouldn't share anything with her.

She dismissed the idea, deciding that not only was Joe very young to be involved with Robespierre, but also a bit too chunky to fit through the attic window — let alone being capable of running about on the roof at night.

Matt was also late appearing. Whilst Philly helped Meg and Puck put out the breakfast buffet on the sideboard in the dining room, she asked about him, trying to sound casual.

'Oh — he's left, Philly. Didn't you know?' said Meg. 'I'm surprised he didn't say goodbye to you.'

'Left . . . ' The mini packet of cornflakes Philly was holding fell to the floor. 'When?'

'This morning, just before you got up. He said he had things to do.'

'Oh well, that solves that problem. I doubt we'll see him again.' She quickly filled her friends in on what Matt had told her the night before.

'The sneak!' growled Meg. 'Oh,

280

Philly, sweetheart, I'm so sorry.' She put her arms around her friend. 'You're well rid of him if you ask me.'

'Yeah, good riddance to bad rubbish,' muttered Puck.

'I thought you both liked him.'

'We did, but now you obviously hate him, we hate him too,' said Meg. 'The rotter.'

'Yeah, he's not worth crying over, sweetheart,' said Puck. 'You can do better.'

'Oh, I doubt it,' said Philly.

'Yeah, I doubt it as well. He was a bit of a peach,' said Puck, winking and clucking the roof of his mouth with his teeth. 'But I'm sure you can do nearly as well. Well probably not even nearly as well, but they do say there's someone for everyone. So . . . yeah, good luck with replacing him.'

'Thank you, Puck, that makes me feel so much better.' Philly couldn't help but smile. Her friends always knew how to cheer her up.

'That's what I'm here for, babe.'

'Have either of you seen Joe this morning?' she asked. 'He's usually first down for breakfast.'

'He went out to do some filming in the grounds,' said Meg. 'He said he wanted some nice winter scenes for the report.'

'Ah, that'll be where he is. If you two can manage here, I might go and look for him. I wanted to ask him something.'

'Yeah, we're about done,' said Puck. 'I'll just fetch the coffee cups.'

'Good. It's time to wrap this up and move on with life, I think,' said Philly. 'After breakfast, we'll gather everyone together for the dénouement, then feed them lunch before they all leave for home. To be honest, I'm willing to accept that Dominique was an alien from another planet, who hitched a ride back home on the same space ship as ET.'

'Works for me,' said Meg.

★   ★   ★

Philly didn't just want to go out and speak to Joe. She wanted to think clearly about Matt, if such a thing were possible. Why had he suddenly left, after refusing to the night before? She began to wonder if everything he told her about his father had been a lie after all, and he really was there all along to try to steal something.

He had turned the finger of suspicion on her, trying to make out she was the one with criminal leanings. When she thought about it, it was a clever trick to play. It put her on the back foot, making it hard for her to continue accusing him, because she was too busy defending herself.

Her heart ached. Despite all her best defences and the doubts she had, she knew she was still in love with him.

She remembered the feeling of inevitability on the day they met. She knew now that only she'd felt that way. This was probably why it had been so easy for him to drive away from her. Well, good riddance to him!

The heavy thought barely reached the hallway ceiling as she put on her thick winter coat. It would take her a long time to get over Matt Cassell. Not just loving him, but her disappointment that he wasn't the man she had believed him to be.

How could she get it so wrong? She always thought she could tell the difference between good people and bad people. Now she wasn't so sure.

Matt's apparent duality had brought to the fore other fears. The fears that she had felt since becoming interested in the mystery of Dominique DuPont's disappearance. Since the very beginning, and for reasons she couldn't fathom, she was convinced it was all connected to her.

As she stepped out of the front door, she shuddered. Not because of the chill in the air, but as if someone had walked over her grave. Suspicions that she had been forcing deep down inside her were coming to the fore. Yet she had no proof . . . only a strong feeling of something not being quite right.

It was partly to do with Mrs Cunningham's newfound realisation that Dominique's accent was put on. It created a flicker of something within Philly. A memory of when she first started drama school and had to practise accents.

She had been no better at it than Meg. Her Yorkshire accent was pretty good, but her French accent always came out sounding Welsh. What was it she had to remember?

Almost as if the memory was afraid to come to the fore, it stayed deep within her, insisting it was irrelevant. It couldn't possibly be part of the jigsaw puzzle that had been forming since she found Robespierre's painting in Dominique's trunk in an attic that neither should have anything to do with. To acknowledge there may be a connection, and complete the puzzle, might be to admit something so painful that she might never recover from it.

She looked around the land. Her

land. The pain subsided a little. Sometimes she found it hard to believe that this beautiful house and park were all hers. Mr Scattergood would no doubt say she was selfish — but even if she sold it, the developers would only turn the house into several apartments selling for a million pounds each.

Why should she not own it all herself, and then maybe pass it on to her children? If she ever had any. She couldn't imagine loving anyone but Matt. He had filled her life so much in such a short time, it already felt empty without him.

15

She saw Joe in the distance and called out to him. 'Have you got anything for me?'

'Not what I thought I had, Philly.' He sat on a wooden bench at the side of the lake, looking at the large viewing screen on his camera.

'Excuse me?'

'Come and sit down and I'll show you. I thought I'd caught your prowler, but it turns out I've only caught a couple of illicit lovers.' He laughed.

'Really? Amongst the guests, you mean?' Philly sat next to him, blowing on her fingers. She really ought to have put her gloves on. 'How fascinating. Do show me.' It was something amusing to take her mind off her troubles.

Joe fiddled with the camera a bit, rewinding it through the events of the night.

'Here, look at this,' he said, pausing the footage at around two-thirty in the morning. 'I found this when I checked the camera on my way back up to bed last night. You can't see much, but you can hear a voice.'

Just as Joe said, there were a couple of figures talking at the top of the stairs, but they had their backs to the camera.

As far as Philly could make out from their size and body forms, one was a man, the other a woman.

'We can't talk now,' said the woman. 'I'll meet you by the lake early in the morning. Say seven o'clock. I always go for a walk before he wakes up.' The man nodded, and they parted company quickly, but neither of them went up to the attic.

'That's Mrs Bennett!' said Philly. 'I'd know her voice anywhere. I wonder if that's Mr Graham? They have become rather close. But I'd have sworn she was devoted to her husband, despite her crushes on random actors.'

'Nah, it's not Mr Graham's voice.

Did you know he used to be a photographer? He did weddings and everything. I love old cameras and he's an interesting man to talk to. Watch this.'

Joe fiddled with the camera again. 'There's nothing else for the rest of the night,' he explained. 'So your prowler must have decided to rest last night. Mrs Bennett met her fancy fella in between you and Matt going up, and me following half an hour later. So I came down here with the camera just before seven. Bit naughty of me, I know, but I couldn't resist finding out who they were.' Joe held the camera up to Philly. 'And here's her secret lover.'

The film showed Mrs Bennett throwing her arms around a man, hugging him tightly. There was very little passion in the embrace, but a lot of love.

'Mr Scattergood! No, it can't be,' said Philly. 'They only met . . . ' She stopped. Of course, it was so obvious. 'No,' she said to Joe. 'They're not

289

lovers. I just think they've known each other for a long time, that's all. I also think I know who the prowler is. We were right. He's been here all along. Mind you, I've no idea how he managed to climb over the roof.'

* * *

Philly said nothing over breakfast. She wanted to try to get Mr Scattergood alone. Despite his brusqueness, she had warmed to the old man because of his affection for her godmother. Unfortunately it also meant that more of the jigsaw puzzle than she ever wanted to see was beginning to appear. But it was better to face it than to pretend it had never happened.

After breakfast, she left Meg and Puck to finish off the dénouement, making sure that Mr Scattergood was sitting safely in a chair in the drawing room. As far as she could tell, he was not about to move. Mrs Bennett seemed very emotional. She kept wiping her eyes, and her husband continually asked her what was wrong.

'Nothing,' she said, sniffing loudly. 'It's just my hormones, that's all.' He seemed happy with that explanation.

Philly went directly to the attic, and then straight to the corner where she had seen the beam of light. Sure enough, she found something she had never noticed before. At the back of the attic was a false door, set into the wooden panels. She pushed it open and peered inside.

There was a light on inside the panelled area, operated by the sort of string one found in a bathroom. That was the light she had seen. The hidden room had other surprises in store. Piled up around the walls in the tiny space were dozens of paintings. Philly didn't know if they were originals or not, but her best bet was that they were.

She would have to phone the police, even though she knew the truth could ruin her. She backed out of the room, and felt something hard sticking into her back.

'I have waited a long time to be able to see them properly,' said Monsieur De Lacey. Philly turned slowly, and saw he held a gun in his hand. 'They belong to me.'

'No,' said Philly firmly. 'They belong to the people you stole them from.'

'They are mine. I knew all along she had deceived me, telling me there were no more paintings left. She tried to pay me off, but I didn't take the money. I knew what was behind here was worth much more. I realised the extent of her lie when I saw your house on television, with Robespierre's fakes on the walls.'

'Let the girl go, Armand,' said a voice from the attic door. 'She's innocent in all this. What's more, she's Robyn's girl.'

'She is merely her goddaughter.' De Lacey turned slightly to look at Mr Scattergood.

'She's still Robyn's girl. The one she gave it all up for.'

'She deceived us both, Robespierre,' said De Lacey. 'She didn't give it all up at all. She merely kept the best for herself. As she always did.'

'That's because she was the one who took all the risks,' said Mr Scattergood taking a few steps towards them.

'Not so,' said Armand.

'She was Dominique, wasn't she?' breathed Philly. 'My godmother was Dominique DuPont.'

'That's right, lass,' said Scattergood. 'She was always young looking, and with a few adjustments to her appearance it was easy to get a place in the school. Armand played her father. As well as being a damn good actor, he also happens to be one of the finest cat burglars ever. Still good at it by the sound of things, though a bit slippery nowadays. He used to send your godmother the stuff disguised in food parcels, I'd copy them, and then we'd replace the original with the fake. All whilst the owners were away living it up on some tropical island with Princess

Margaret and the Aga Khan. Half the time they never even noticed the change. Then we'd sell the originals to buyers who weren't too fussy about where they got their art from.'

'The dates in the tower were the times you met, weren't they?' asked Philly.

Mr Scattergood nodded. 'Yes, and when I was caught that time, I deliberately told the police the truth, knowing that they wouldn't believe me. I had met a man and a beautiful woman who gave me money. Dominique — your godmother — and De Lacey. I just fudged knowing their names. It was a double bluff that worked.'

Philly turned to De Lacey. 'You hurt your ankle, falling from the roof.' She struggled to keep her voice calm. He still had the gun pointed at her. 'So you had to pretend you'd fallen downstairs to explain why you were limping.'

'You are as clever as your godmother,' said De Lacey. 'And as greedy. Keeping the paintings to yourself.'

'No!' Philly exclaimed. 'I didn't know about them until today — or the secret room, for that matter. I guessed there was something hidden up here, but I didn't know what. I'm going to phone the police and they can find the original owners.'

'No!' De Lacey waved the gun about. 'I need the money. I'm an old man now and not able to do what I used to do. It damn near killed me climbing over your roof. I cannot earn a living.'

'Yes you can,' said Philly. 'You could do something honest. Work in a bank, pack groceries, work in a burger bar. No one has to be a criminal.'

De Lacey laughed. 'You foolish, self-satisfied girl. Perhaps you will not be quite so self-righteous when you realise what paid for your education and your place in drama school. Your godmother never worked a day in her life either. She was not born to it.'

'She could have been,' said Scatter-good. 'She just never tried. Don't think too harshly of her, Philomela. It was drummed into her from a very early age that she had to keep this house, no matter what.

'She met Armand here in France and he taught her how she could do that. When she came here to the school, their usual forger had just died. She saw the work I'd done for the church Nativity and approached me. I was only fourteen, so you can imagine how excited I was when this beautiful, sophisticated woman involved me in her exciting plot. It was a real adventure for me.' Mr Scattergood smiled. It was the first time Philly had seen him do so.

'Put the gun down, Armand,' he continued. 'You're not going to shoot the girl. We're not about that. We never were. Our rule was always that no one got hurt. Only the rich suffered, and they could afford it. Remember.'

'I remember your ideals, Robespierre, but they were never mine. You always wanted to strike back at the upper classes. Not that it stopped you taking your cut when the money was shared out. I don't have your ideals, though. I don't care if this girl gets hurt.'

'You always were the odd one out, De Lacey,' growled Scattergood. 'I do care about the girl, and so does everyone standing outside this attic door.' Scattergood stepped aside a little, to show the group of guests. The Reverend and Mrs Cunningham were at the head of them, clinging together, their kind faces full of concern. 'When I saw you follow the girl up, I told them to come with me and see a real dénouement.'

'Then I have nothing to lose,' said De Lacey. 'Because I'm not spending the rest of my life in a prison cell. I want what is due to me.'

What happened next was something of a blur. Philly became aware of one of the trunks opening, and a figure emerging from it. He struck Monsieur De Lacey on the head and knocked the gun from his hand.

'I don't know about what's due to you,' said Matt, 'but you'll certainly get what's coming to you.'

People rushed into the attic to surround De Lacey and ensure he couldn't get away.

'Matt?'

'Hi, darling.'

'Puck and Meg said you'd gone.'

'Yeah, sorry about that. I asked them to lie. I've been here all along. I had a feeling something was going to happen today.'

'You did?'

'Well, it's the last day the house is open to guests, so I figured our prowler would be getting desperate.'

After that, everything became chaotic as the police arrived. As Mr Scattergood was being led away in handcuffs, Philly went up to him. 'I want to thank you, Mr . . . I'm sorry, I don't even know what to call you now.'

'Harry. Harry Johnson,' he said. His sister came to stand by his side.

'I thought I'd lost him forever,' she

said, sniffing loudly. 'But now I've got a brother again.'

'Probably not when they take me to jail, sweetheart,' said Harry ruefully.

'Well at least I'll know where you are for a change,' said Mrs Bennett, smiling through her tears.

'Thank you, Harry,' said Philly, reaching up to kiss his cheek. 'I'll tell the police about how you tried to save me. With any luck it will go towards your defence.'

'I appreciate that, lass, thank you. I knew it would catch up with me eventually, though. A man can't run away from his past forever. I'm glad it's over now.'

'You'd better come with us too, Miss,' said one of the policemen. 'We've a lot of questions we want to ask you and your two friends.'

'But we didn't know anything about it,' protested Philly.

Her pleas and those of everyone present were ignored as Philly, Meg and Puck were taken to the police station.

As Philly was led away, she heard Mr Graham's new love interest say, 'The police are very convincing, aren't they?'

Another lady said, 'Best murder mystery weekend ever!'

★ ★ ★

'I can hardly believe it,' said Mrs Cunningham, pouring Philly a cup of tea in the cluttered living room of the Cunningham's bungalow. 'All this time, I've had nightmares about Dominique coming to serious harm — and all along she was your godmother in disguise.'

'I'm so sorry.' Philly wrung her hands.

'Oh no, don't be. It isn't your fault, and I'm glad the police finally accepted that. It was ridiculous to think otherwise.' Mrs Cunningham smiled. 'I think I guessed, you know, when you sang *No Regrets*. Your phrasing in the French parts were so much like Dominique's.'

'My godmother coached me in a

French accent when I was at drama school,' said Philly. 'I suppose I must have picked up her bad habits.'

'Yes, you did rather. Fancy Mr Scattergood turning out to be Robespierre and Harry Johnson! I think that's far too many aliases for one person, don't you?'

Philly smiled a little sadly. 'Yes, and I still don't know what to call him. It's a shame really. I keep thinking that if my godmother hadn't corrupted him, he might have become a really great artist in time.'

'He was very young and impressionable, that's for certain,' the older lady mused.

'I'm still struggling with it all,' said Philly. 'The idea that my whole life is a lie, paid for by organised crime.'

'That's hardly your fault, dear, and it doesn't change the honest person that you are. I think we have to give your godmother some credit for that. She could easily have corrupted you too, but for some reason she chose not to.'

'She still lived on the earnings from stolen paintings.'

'Yes, that is a problem, but it's not your problem, Philly. The truth is out there now, as they say on *The X-Files*, and that's for the best. Oh, I do like Agent Mulder, don't you?' She smiled.

'You are incorrigible,' said Philly, laughing. 'Thank you for still allowing me into your home.'

'Why wouldn't I? You must stop taking the guilt of everything on your own shoulders, dear girl. You have done absolutely nothing wrong.'

'I feel as if everyone is judging me, wondering whether it's possible that I was involved. I even ask myself how I could have spent time with my godmother without ever guessing what was going on.'

'When she pretended to be Dominique, she made sure no one guessed, Philly. She was a clever woman. It's only now, with hindsight and a lot of information I didn't have at the time, that I can see she wasn't quite right as

302

Dominique. Even when I had misgivings, I took her as I found her. You'd even less reason to suspect her. Presumably she was a woman who was kind to you soon after you lost your parents. Children are just grateful to be loved and cared for. It doesn't matter what else their parent or guardian does.'

Mrs Cunningham took another sip of tea.

'When I was a teacher I met parents who seemed absolutely awful. Certainly not people I would trust with a child. Yet when I saw them with their children, it was clear they wanted the best for them. They may not have always gone the right way about it, but the love was genuine.'

'I don't know that my godmother did love me,' said Philly. 'She was stuck with me, that's all.'

'Now you're just feeling sorry for yourself for the sake of it,' said Mrs Cunningham with uncustomary brusqueness. Philly knew that she meant well. The former teacher continued in a softer tone, 'Why don't you invite that nice young Matt over? I'm sure he can put you straight.'

'I haven't seen him since the day we were arrested,' said Philly, glumly. 'He went back to America to tell his dad what happened. He hasn't called or anything.'

'I see.' Mrs Cunningham smiled secretively.

'So I guess he did just want to find out the truth after all.'

'Well, you know how the saying about fat ladies and singing goes. I wouldn't rule him out yet, Philly. What are you doing for Christmas lunch today?'

'Meg and Puck have been invited to his mum's for the day. I've been asked to go too, but I don't know if I'm very good company at the moment.'

'It'll be much better than you sitting up at that house all alone and miserable. If you change your mind, Andrew and I would be delighted to welcome you here. We'll be eating around two o'clock.'

'Thank you.' Philly stood up and leaned over to give Mrs Cunningham a kiss. 'I am so glad I met you and your husband. You've both been wonderful to me.'

'Well, I care what happens to Dominique's girl, even if Dominique wasn't really Dominique. All the time I was in the house over that weekend, I felt that she was sending me signals, asking me to take care of you. I shan't let you disappear, you can count on it.'

Philly choked back a sob. 'I shan't go anywhere, I promise.' She went to the door and opened it, turning back. 'Aunt Robyn didn't tell me much about her life, for obvious reasons. But she did occasionally talk about a wonderful teacher that she once knew. I think I know now who she was talking about.'

'Thank you for that, child,' said Mrs Cunningham, wiping a teary eye. 'Merry Christmas.'

'And a Merry Christmas to you too.'

16

Actually what Philly had told Mrs Cunningham was not strictly true. She had been in touch with a developer about selling the house. It seemed to be the best thing to do. She could cut her losses, pay off her crippling business loan, and maybe have enough to buy a nice flat in which to live. She had promised Meg and Puck she would choose one with two bedrooms so they had somewhere to live too.

She loved Bedlington Hall, but she didn't like the associations or the recent intrusion. For days after the mystery weekend, the newspapers and television had covered the story, bringing photographers to her front door, and causing the phone to ring incessantly — so much so that she had finally had enough and unplugged it from the wall.

Things had quietened down a little,

with other news overtaking the story of her godmother's gang, but there was still the feeling that her home had been sullied. The bricks with which it was built were bought with the proceeds of crime.

'I'm sorry, Aunt Robyn,' murmured Philly, standing looking over the lake on a frosty Christmas morning. 'I don't believe the house should be kept at *any* costs.'

Nevertheless, she felt a deep ache in her heart at letting the house go, as if she had somehow failed her godmother. But it had been a terrible burden to place upon someone.

In many ways she pitied Robyn, imagining how much that message must have been drummed into her by her parents when she was a child. At least Philly had been saved much of that. Only her godmother's deathbed plea had put an obligation on Philly. She wondered whether Robyn had resisted saying it until that last moment, and was suddenly overcome by her parents' teaching as she died.

Philly could hear the church bells ringing in the distance, and scent the aroma of roasting turkey filling the air. Perhaps she would walk back down to the Cunninghams after all.

She strolled back up to the house, noticing that the smell of cooking grew stronger as she got nearer.

'There you are,' said Meg, when she opened the front door. 'We wondered what had happened to you, until we phoned Mrs Cunningham and she said you'd been there.'

'I thought you were at Puck's mum's.'

'They had another fall-out about him not getting a proper job.' Meg rolled her eyes heavenward. 'Same old, same old. Besides, there's no way we'd have left you on your own today.'

Philly ran to hug her friend. 'Thank you!'

'We've invited the Cunninghams up to lunch,' said Puck, coming from the kitchen wearing his favourite pinny. 'I hope you don't mind, but Rachel and Joe are coming too. They were too busy to go home for Christmas.'

'Of course I don't mind.'

'Oh,' said Puck, grinning. 'And there's a present for you in the drawing room.'

'I thought we'd agreed on no presents,' said Philly, feeling alarmed. 'Because we're all broke.'

'Yeah, well luckily we didn't have to pay for this one. Go on, before it gets cold.'

Meg punched Puck playfully. 'Behave. Come on, back to the kitchen with you. Dinner won't cook itself.'

'At last,' cried Puck, 'after all those years staring at the cooker with a blank expression, she realises.'

Laughing, Philly went into the drawing room, where someone had lit a lovely warm fire. And standing in front of the fire was Matt, looking utterly gorgeous in a thick Aran sweater.

'Hi,' he said.

'Hi.' Philly was overwhelmed by a

rush of feelings for him.

'How are you?'

'Great, thanks. And you?'

'Yeah great . . . Philly . . . ' He held out his arms, and she threw herself into them. They kissed, and for the first time, Philly was able to let go of all her doubts and fears.

'I thought I was never going to see you again,' she whispered, teary-eyed. 'After everything . . . '

'You don't get rid of me that easily. I had to go home and explain to my folks why I wouldn't be spending Christmas with them. So they insisted I spent a few days with them first. You don't mind, do you?'

'Oh no. I'm so glad you're here. I wanted to talk to you. I've been so stupid, Matt.' Philly rested her head on his chest, relishing the feel of his strong arms around her.

'No, you haven't. *I*'ve been stupid.'

'Well, yes,' she said, impishly. 'You were a bit more stupid than I was.'

'And after I'd brought you a present!'

310

said Matt, laughing.

'You're a wonderful present. I love you.'

'Well, that's the best present I've ever had,' he murmured, pausing to kiss her passionately. 'I love you too. I have loved you since the day we met. Even when I thought you were a sultry thief. When the police took you away I was busily planning how to break you out of prison.'

'Were you?'

'Yep, it involved a lot of cake and several files.'

'I love you for even thinking of it.'

'In the end I just told them that you were the most wonderful, honest girl I'd ever met.'

'You did?'

'Yep. Luckily our company are well known to the police in Britain. We've helped on a few of their cases, so they took my word for it.'

'Just as well they don't know about the Mona Lisa I stashed in my bedroom then.'

'You won't need a Mona Lisa,' said Matt. He led her by the hand to one of the sofas. On it was a big brown package. 'Here,' he said. 'Unwrap it.'

Philly eagerly did as he suggested.

'The Robespierre painting!' she said, frowning.

'I know, technically it's not a present, because it already belongs to you,' said Matt. 'I have brought you a proper present but I wanted you to see this first.'

'But it will have to go to the police, darling,' said Philly. 'With all the others.'

'No, it won't. I took it to Scattergood . . . Harry . . . whatever his darn name is, in prison, and he told me all about it. Your godmother commissioned it, so it definitely belongs to you, as the one who inherited her estate.'

'It's not a copy?' said Philly.

'No, it's the real deal, and probably worth a lot of money what with all the recent publicity. It might even help towards the upkeep of the house.

Anyway, he told me all about it. The full title is *The Robyn Watches The Nightingale.*' His words brought a shiver to Philly's spine. She couldn't decide if it was a good shiver or a bad one.

As if sensing her conflicted emotions, Matt put his arms around her again and they stood looking at the picture together.

'Darling, the little figure in the painting in the red anorak is you, with the bird representing your godmother, Robyn. Scattergood said to notice how the bird is looking away from the house, because she has found a new purpose. A new reason to live. The little girl who was given into her keeping.'

'Oh, Matt.' Philly started to cry. He held her for a long time.

'I'll never sell it,' she said eventually. 'You don't mind, do you? It's just that I'd rather sell the house than the painting. It shows, I think, that she had some good in her.'

'Why on earth would I mind? You

don't think I care about the money, do you?'

'No — well, not in that way. I know your family are well off, but I'm broke. I suppose having some money would have evened the score a bit. I have nothing to offer you.'

'How can you say that? You have yourself. That's all I want. It's all I've ever wanted. I love you, Philly, and if you come to me with holes in your shoes and no clothes on your back, I'll still love you.'

'I'm not quite that bad. I could get a job — a proper job, like Puck's mother is always nagging him to do.'

'Philly, I can help with the house. You can carry on here.'

'No!' Philly shook her head and pulled away from him a little. 'It isn't worth it, Matt. You were right when you said that it's people who make a house. Well the people who make this house are Meg and Puck and you. It's the love and friendship we give and receive from each other that matters. And we can have that anywhere, can't we?'

'You're wrong, of course,' said Matt.

'You mean we can't have that anywhere?'

'I mean that it's you who makes this house. We're just very lucky that you allow us to share it.'

'I'm the lucky one,' said Philly, kissing him again.

★ ★ ★

Christmas dinner was the happiest that Philly had ever known. She had all her friends and the man she loved with her. What more could any girl want?

'Puck and I are going to get married,' said Meg excitedly, over dessert.

'I thought you couldn't afford it,' replied Rachel Jenson. 'I know, because I've had mum on the phone to me, moaning that Puck still hasn't got a job.'

'We decided that if we waited until we could afford it, we'd never marry,' said Puck. 'Besides, my biological clock is ticking. If I don't have a baby soon, I'll be too old.' Everyone laughed.

'Not only that,' said Puck, switching to an impersonation of Morgan Freeman, 'Being inside changes a man. He realises what's important. Like love and babies, and not being chatted up by a tattooed man called Big Herbie.'

'Puck, you were there for two hours,' said Philly. 'In a police cell. There were no Big Herbies at the police station.'

'Maybe not on your block,' said Puck. 'But down on C Block things got pretty hairy for a while, and I'm not just talking about Big Herbie's chest. Anyway, seriously, I love Meg more than anything in the world, and I'm going to get a proper job as a chef, so I can support her and all our babies.'

'That's wonderful news,' said Mrs Cunningham.

'Yes — and we'd be grateful if the Reverend there would come out of retirement and perform the ceremony.'

'I'd be absolutely delighted,' said Andrew Cunningham.

'It's a great idea,' said Matt. 'Let's raise a toast to Puck and Meg.' The room was filled with a chorus of congratulations.

'But that reminds me, Philly,' Matt went on. 'I forgot to give you my other present.' He put his hands in his pocket and pulled out a small box. 'We could make it a double wedding, if the Reverend has no objections.'

'I don't think it's my decision,' said Andrew, smiling.

'You want to *marry* me?' said Philly, unbelieving.

'Of course I do. Well, I have to do something to save you from a life of crime!'

'How do you know I won't corrupt you?'

'There is an answer to that,' said Matt, 'but I'm not going to say it on Christmas Day and with the Reverend and his good lady listening in. Will you marry me, Philomela?'

'Yes!'

More toasts followed, and everyone

got into the party spirit.

'Well, Rachel,' said Joe, coughing. 'Whilst we're on the subject . . . '

'Not in this lifetime,' said Rachel. She blew him a kiss. 'But maybe when you grow up a bit, hey?'

'That's as good as a yes to me.'

★   ★   ★

'Ladies and gentlemen,' said Matt, standing on the stairs of Bedlington Hall looking down at a crowd of guests. 'Welcome to our second Mistletoe Mystery weekend. You will witness the unfolding of the fascinating story of schoolgirl Dominique DuPont, and the secret life she led at Bedlington Hall School.

'As a special treat, on Saturday night we will be screening the award-winning documentary by Rachel Jenson, in which she talks to master forger, Robespierre, about his role in the crime. You will also have the opportunity to meet and talk to retired teacher,

Meredith Cunningham, who taught at the school.'

Not long after Christmas day the previous year, when Philly remembered to plug the phone back in, they were inundated with people wanting to visit the house and find out about what went on there. As such, nearly every weekend since had been booked up. Not only that, but Philly soon learned just how much film companies were willing to pay to use Bedlington Hall in their dramas. It hadn't only helped with the upkeep of the hall, but also allowed them to hire more actors and helpers for the murder mystery weekends.

'Robespierre is my brother,' said Irene Bennett proudly, nudging the woman next to her. 'He's still in prison, but I don't think that's fair myself. He saved that girl's life, you know, so it's possible he might be out soon. There she is.' Mrs Bennett pointed to Philly. 'The pretty blue-eyed one with the baby in her arms. The handsome American on the stairs is her husband.

Oh, and look, there's Meg dressed as Dominique DuPont. She's married to Puck, the chef. He does that programme on telly, Cooking With Puck.' Mrs Bennett paused for breath. 'Mind you, whilst I'm sure this year's entertainment will be good, it won't beat last year. There were real guns and everything. I mean, who would bring a gun to a murder mystery weekend? It's beyond me, really.'

Philly stifled a giggle, and looked adoringly at her husband, whilst little one-month old Robyn lay peacefully in her arms. Matt finished his welcoming speech and went down to stand at her side while the guests climbed the stairs to their rooms.

'I see that the Nightingale is watching the Robyn,' he whispered softly.

'Yes,' murmured Philly. 'And I'm never going to let her, or you, out of my sight.'

'And I'll be watching both of you.'

She followed Matt's eyes as he looked up at the ceiling and grinned. A

We do hope that you have enjoyed reading this large print book.

Did you know that all of our titles are available for purchase?

We publish a wide range of high quality large print books including:
Romances, Mysteries, Classics
General Fiction
Non Fiction and Westerns

Special interest titles available in large print are:
The Little Oxford Dictionary
Music Book, Song Book
Hymn Book, Service Book

Also available from us courtesy of Oxford University Press:
Young Readers' Dictionary
(large print edition)
Young Readers' Thesaurus
(large print edition)

For further information or a free brochure, please contact us at:
Ulverscroft Large Print Books Ltd.,
The Green, Bradgate Road, Anstey,
Leicester, LE7 7FU, England.
Tel: (00 44) 0116 236 4325
Fax: (00 44) 0116 234 0205

sprig of mistletoe was strategically placed right above them. Oblivious to the guests around them and mindful of the precious bundle in her arms, Matt kissed Philly passionately.

'Merry Christmas, darling.'

THE END